THE
WOMAN
ON THE BEAST

TREASURES IN JARS OF CLAY

THE
WOMAN
ON THE BEAST

Revelatio 17: The enemy that's causing the church so much pain.

VERONICA BELLAMY

TATE PUBLISHING
AND ENTERPRISES, LLC

Published by Tate Publishing & Enterprises, LLC
127 E. Trade Center Terrace | Mustang, Oklahoma 73064 USA
1.888.361.9473 | www.tatepublishing.com

Tate Publishing is committed to excellence in the publishing industry. The company reflects the philosophy established by the founders, based on Psalm 68:11,
"The Lord gave the word and great was the company of those who published it."

Book design copyright © 2014 by Tate Publishing, LLC. All rights reserved.
Cover design by Jim Villaflores
Interior design by Joana Quilantang

Published in the United States of America

ISBN: 978-1-63122-128-6
Fiction / Christian / General
14.03.04

I am a letter from Christ. And I will be known and read by everybody with the spirit of the living God. This book is from my heart.

—2 Corinthians 3:3
(Father-Son-Holy Spirit)

DEDICATION

To the love of my life, the Father-Son-Holy Spirit
To my husband, Jerry Bellamy Sr.
To my son, Jerry J. Bellamy Jr.
To my parents, Grace and Harold Rice
(To Joseph White and Belinda White)
To my sisters, Tonya Rice and Nathalene Rice
To my brothers, Reginald Rice and Harold Rice Jr.

I would like to thank God for my family and their support while away on my journey, standing by me, cheering me on, giving me the love I needed to carry and guide me through. I thank my Father for the vessels that allowed him in, regarding the financial support during my journey. I also give thanks to my husband's family for all their prayers.

THANK YOU, LORD!

ACKNOWLEDGMENTS

Thanking God for—
The Missionaries on my Journey
The Fellowship of the Cross
Brother Matthew
Brother Travis
Lily of the Valley
Pastor Morris Green
Moms in Touch

CONTENTS

My life began like this:

The prince of this world (darkness) petitioned the prince of the heavens (light), and he said, "I know the time is near. So we need to DNA (do not answer) all of our children. One by one will they need to be tested.

The prince of darkness said, "I want to identify mine and take count. And I know you want to identify yours also, and take count. So when the prince of darkness petitioned the heavens, Michael the archangel (who is like God) came down, and he looked around—through and through, church by church, home by home—and then Michael the archangel spoke four words: LET THE TESTING BEGIN!

The Lord put a warrant out for my arrest. My soul is what he wanted. I was placed on heaven's most wanted list.

"Clean or unclean?" he asked.

Then I watched as a scroll rolled out, and it read, "Find her! Snatch everything from her, leaving her naked and unclothed, powerless, helpless, and weak. Leave her with no fig leaves to cover up with, but do not touch a hair on her head" (Luke 21:18).

"She will be ashamed, and dread the nakedness, but this is the Lord Almighty, and I am coming down, and I will be walking around in the cool of day" (Genesis 3:7–8). "Now let the weeping and mourning and the woes begin." And so they did…

This is my story.

I HAD A DREAM

In my dream, I was running through some woods—running for dear life. I had no clue to why I was running or who was chasing me. All I could hear were loud sounds of footsteps coming after me. They had the sounds of giants and footprints of that of an animal, and they were getting closer and closer to me. I was losing strength but I kept on running, when all of a sudden something or someone caught up with me. I fell, face to the ground, wondering what or who was chasing me and why.

As I was lying on the ground, I could see the shadows of my aggressors. I looked up and *Oh, my God!* There were three creatures standing over me that had the appearance of super humans—at least fifteen-feet-tall giants with long arms like tree branches. As they stood over me, they swung their arms from the north, the south, the east, and the west.

They seemed very strong, positioning themselves as though they were getting ready to wage war against me. I screamed! And as I looked, I saw that the creatures were smiling at me. The more loudly I screamed, the more they smiled, as if they enjoyed my terror. I looked closely at their faces and I noticed that each had the face of a man, hair like a woman, and the body of an animal. They were growling at me, making the sounds of wolves howling and growling in the air as though they were getting hungry and I was the prey.

I cried, "Oh, my God! What do I do?"

Then I heard a voice say, "Do not let your heart be troubled; trust in God" (John 14:1). I sat quietly trusting God, yet watching the creatures. Though they never said a word, neither did they take their eyes off me. Lying in fear, I put my hands over my eyes, not wanting them to see that I was gazing at them. I spread my fingers apart to look at what they were doing, because the creatures were suddenly very quiet, looking and watching everything I did. Then I noticed that all three began to mock me. All of these creatures had their hands over their eyes with their fingers spread apart, smiling at me.

Wow! I thought. *This doesn't look good.*

So I tried to get up slowly, thinking I had a chance to get away. When I stood, all of a sudden the three creatures attacked me. One of them was biting my ears while the tallest one was sniffing me out and smelling my hair, strand by strand.

As he smelled under my arms, my legs, and even my feet, I became curious about the smell he was wanting. I asked the Lord, "Why does he smell me?"

And I heard a voice answer, "He is looking for the smell of death (sin) and as long as you pray, he will only be able to smell the fragrance of life (the aroma from heaven). The smell of death is what he craves. Be still, daughter!" So I decided to lie still and wait upon the

Lord, just praying and crying to him and only moving my mouth. As I began my prayer, immediately the creatures stopped smelling me and looked only at my mouth, taking note of everything I did, and every move I made they were watching me.

My Lord, was I frightened! But I was yet lying still until the creature began to place his mouth over mine, trying to suck all the life out of me by putting his whole mouth over my mouth. I was unable to breathe the foul smell from his breath, which was causing me to pass out. It was the smell of death, and it was overpowering me. Fear crept into me quickly, and I screamed louder and louder. I did not know what else to do. I could hardly breathe.

Finally, I decided to follow the instruction of the Father's will to be still. I lay there quietly trying to catch my breath when all of a sudden the last creature tried to gouge my eyes out of my head. I fought as hard as I could to save my eyes and my ears, crying out to the Father as I fought the creatures.

"Lord!" I begged. "What do these creatures want with my eyes and ears? Protect me, oh Lord!"

I cried, and I heard a voice saying, "No eyes have seen, no ears have heard, no mind has conceived what God has prepared for those who love him" (1 Corinthians 2:9).

I stopped fighting, and all of a sudden the creatures stopped beating me. I fell to the ground, tired from the fight, just lying there. Then the last creature—the most vicious of them all—grabbed me by the feet and dragged me backward through the woods. He went with me running, moving so fast that the branches from the trees would break at the sound of his foot. After running so long with me, the creature took off in midair with me with the other creatures following. He swung from tree to tree, branch by branch, until finally we landed and ended up at an old house in the back of the woods.

Through the doors of the old house the creatures went with me. As we entered the house, I noticed a family there. *Wait a minute*, I thought. *This looks like my family!* I looked again closely, and it was my family indeed, all sitting quietly, doing what they do best—watching television!

"Oh no, Lord!" I cried. "Please don't let the creatures beat up my family, and *what* are they doing here?" I prayed and I cried for them, but they could neither hear nor see me or the creatures. I cried, weeping out loud to the Lord, and one of the creatures picked me up and threw me across his shoulders. Up the stairs he carried me while leaving the other two creatures downstairs with my family. I was so scared that I did not know what to do.

Then the creature placed me on the bed and closed the door of the room, leaving me all alone. I sat on the edge of the bed, exhausted and afraid of what was happening to my family downstairs. "Lord!" I prayed. "I petition the heavens and ask if you are willing to please tell me who these giant creatures are? And what do they want with me?"

"Quiet!" the Lord said, and I let the Spirit speak. I closed my eyes and listened to the Spirit of the Lord. He told me that these giant creatures were demons.

"They are called heroes of old men of renown" (Genesis 6:4). The Lord then said, "They are Nephilims who have been around a long time, even before the flood. They are very dangerous."

The Lord continued, "You must be very careful of them. These men are springs without water and mists driven by a storm. Blackest darkness is reserved for them" (2 Peter 2:17).

"They are God haters," the Spirit said. "You will need strength and faith to get you through. You will need to take courage, daughter, and not faint."

I got on my knees and asked, "Lord! What do they want with me?"

And then the Lord spoke, "They want to wage war against you."

"War!" I asked the Lord. "Why? What did I do wrong, Lord? What sin did I commit to deserve this?"

And the Lord said, "Listen to the Spirit. Listen closely, my child, for if you live according to the sinful nature, you will die. If by the Spirit you put to death the misdeeds of the body you will live, because those who are led by the spirit of God are sons of God. For you did not receive a spirit that makes you a slave again to fear, but you receive the spirit of sonship. And by him we cry, 'Abba! Father,' the Spirit himself testifies with our spirit that we are God's children. Now if we are children then we are heirs. Heirs of God and coheirs with Christ" (Romans 8:13–17).

I got off my knees and I looked up to heaven, and I spoke, "Abba, Father, help me! What do I do now?"

And the Spirit spoke. He said, "They want your family, each one of them."

Then the Spirit spoke again. He said, "God will give you grace. Humble yourself, therefore, under God's mighty hand that he may lift you up in due time. Cast all your anxiety on him because he cares for you. Be self-controlled and alert. Your enemy, the devil, prowls around like a roaring lion looking for something to devour. Resist him by standing firm in faith because you know that your brothers throughout the world are undergoing the same kind of suffering. God opposes the proud but gives grace to the humble" (1 Peter 5: 6–9).

I prayed to the Lord. I was in a state of confusion. I cried loudly, "Lord! How do I war against demons that I can see? Not just one but three, and they are big and strong. Lord!" I cried. "You say have faith. But did you see what they did to me back in the woods? Lord! They mocked me, and then they tried to remove my eyes and take my ears from seeing and hearing your voice. Lord, I am no match for them!"

While I was still speaking, I heard a voice saying, "And the God of all grace who called you to his external glory in Christ after you have suffered a little while will himself restore you, and make you strong firm and steadfast" (1 Peter 5:10).

I was still in the dark to what the Father was doing. After all, I could only see what my eyes were showing me. There I was in an old house with what I now knew as demons downstairs with my family, and I was told I would have to face them. I already knew what they were capable of doing to a man. It was hard for me not to fear. After all, I could see them, but I could not see the Father. I could only hear him—the voice of the Lord—which was all I had. I did not understand.

I thought, *How can I fight these demons for my family? What weapons can I use to fight with?* I looked around, and the room was empty with nothing in it but a bed. *Wow!* I thought ironically. *This is great. A woman! I am a woman fighting for my whole entire family, even fighting for my husband, a man without a weapon to use. No weapon in sight. How unfair is this, Lord!*

And the voice of the Lord answered, "You need to learn your power and your strength. You need to understand what has been given to you from the beginning. I did not create the man for the woman, but the woman for the man for this reason, and because of the angels the woman should have a sign of authority on her head (1 Corinthians 11: 9–10) representing the glory of the man, and the man represent the image and glory of God as the head of her life."

"You are the Gospel," the Lord said, "and you will need to learn how to fight and go to war! And yes, for your entire family—war!"

"Lord, did you say war? In this world, Lord?" I cried. "We are struggling, and things are not looking good. The enemy is gaining strength in my home. How do I war against them?"

I heard a voice say, "Daughter, look up to the hills where comes your help. Be confident that you belong to Christ, for though we live in the world, we do not wage war. As the world does, the weapons we fight with are not the weapons of the world."

"On the contrary, they have divine power to demolish arguments and every pretension that sets itself up against the knowledge of God, and we take captive every thought to make it obedient to Christ. And we will be ready to punish every act of disobedience once your obedience is complete. You are looking only on the surface of things" (2 Corinthians 10:3–7).

I thought, *Okay, Holy Spirit, if ever there was a time of need, it is now.* I remembered that the Holy Spirit was given to me by Christ. He is my messenger and my counselor, and right now at this present time I needed him, and I needed a quick message. I could hear rumbling downstairs and loud thumps. I heard the sound of war breaking out.

"Lord," I cried. "Please help my family!"

LET ME OUT

I had no idea how to begin my prayer. I closed my eyes. I said, "Holy Spirit, I am weak. I see no hope in my situation."

And the Spirit said, "But if we hope for what we do not yet have, we wait for it patiently. In the same way the Spirit help us in our weakness. We do not know what we ought to pray for, but the Spirit himself intercedes for us with groans that words cannot express, and for he who searches, one heart knows the mind of the Spirit, because the Spirit intercedes for the saints in accordance with God's will" (Romans 8:25–27).

I then asked, "Lord, open the doors of this house and let me out!" Yes, I wanted out! I decided I was going to leave.

And immediately I heard the voice of the Lord saying, "Ask and it will be given to you; seek and you will find; knock, and the doors shall be opened to you" (Matthew 7:7).

Suddenly all the windows and doors opened. I was let out. I asked no questions. Through the window I went. I jumped out and ran as fast as I could. Nothing would stop me. As I was running, I looked down and noticed what looked like a stick—just a long stick of wood. It began to move and followed me I ran faster. It moved with great speed and slowly turned itself into a male snake and gazed at me. *Wow!* I screamed as it stood up by my side, sizzling at me with his tongue. I screamed again, and his body began changing colors to camouflage himself.

He blended in with my clothing and made himself the same color and the same height as I, looking just like me. He had my face on his face as he stood long, colorful, and tall. I did not know what to do, seeing that snake running side by side with me, staring at my eyes, with my face. I thought, *Lord, if you would bless me to make it through this without getting bitten, you would have had mercy upon me.*

This was the most ruthless and cruel-looking snake I had ever seen. Oh my! Was he crafty, masquerading himself to look like me! Dangerous is what he was, and he was in my midst. I knew one wrong move would be deadly for me. I knew the serpent was the enemy chasing me. So I kept running, trying not to show fear, and the snake slid his tongue out at my flesh, trying to touch me with his poison.

He spoke, "I will always stand side by side with you, because of the beginning." He slid his forked tongue out of his mouth, darkness upon it. He added, "There will always be enmity between you and me; between the children of God and the children of my offspring, the devil" (Genesis 3:13–15).

I cried, "Lord! Lord! Have mercy on me! Get this evil away from me. He is speaking darkness over my life. Lord! Did you hear him? He hates me! My Lord! Please help me."

The snake spat at me, and I spat back at him, speaking to him, "The Messiah will crush your head."

The snake spoke again and said, "Your children will give you pain, and your husband will rule over you. You will hate the day you were born."

"Stop!" I screamed. "Go away! Please get away from me."

He spoke again. "Pick your poison. Will it be your husband, or the children I will attack by eating at their flesh. Which one do you love the most? Who shall it be?" he asked.

I screamed louder and louder, "Get back! Get back! Leave me alone!"

And then I spoke boldly, "I will be obedient to my Christ. I will be wise about what is good and innocent about what is evil. The God of peace will soon crush Satan under my feet" The grace of our Lord Jesus is with me" (Romans 16:20).

After I spoke, I heard a voice saying, "I saw Satan fall like lightning from heaven. I have given you the authority to trample on snakes and scorpions, and to overcome all the power of the enemy. Nothing will harm you" (Luke 10:18–19).

"Hold your head up!" the voice shouted, and I then began looking up and not down. I spoke to the enemy as I ran side by side with him. I spoke boldly.

"Satan!" I called out. "I demolish every intent of evil with the authority and power of Jesus Christ my Savior. Leave!"

And the snake left, and I looked. There at the end of the woods, surprisingly, was a car. I ran to the driver's side, and into the car I went, amazed that I actually made it through the woods without harm. I just sat there for a minute, thinking about all the things I had been through in my life—storm after storm, fighting demon after demon, sometimes getting hurt while at war with the enemy, constantly engaged in battle after battle. Was I tired!

So I decided to start the car and drive, thanking God for getting me out of that house unharmed. I prayed, "Lord! I don't know what I am walking away from, but I do know that you are my water walker and that I should be still." As I was praying, God gave me a vision that began with me sitting upon the edge of my bed. The last thing I remembered was locking the front doors of my house and walking away from everything.

TOO LATE TO GO BACK

I cried, "Lord! Wait a minute—did I just walk away from my family? Are they going to be okay? Lord! Are they still in that house?"

The Lord replied, "Yes! They are there—all of them. You left them, and they are all still surrounded with the Nephilims."

"Oh my God!" I cried. "I've got to go back!" And as I turned the car around, all of a sudden everything disappeared right before my eyes—all the trees, the woods, and even the old house was gone. It was just me and the voice of the Lord, with only one way to go. All the roads were gone except the one on which I was traveling. The Lord had taken everything away from me, even my family, and I could only go straight with my eyes looking ahead of me. I started to drive, and I asked the Lord, "Where now?

I now knew that God was in control, and the Lord answered: "Now! Wherever I want to take you, you will go. I am the director of your path. Although listening to the Father speaking, knowing that I had just left everything behind, my heart was fearful. Yet I knew God makes no mistakes. I cried, and began pleading with the Father not to separate me from my family. But it seems he was not listening to me. I started to feel as if I was losing control over my situation and began to panic. I tried to unlock the car door to jump out, but I realized the Father had secured my path. Every door was shut and locked! No going back…

This time I had no choice but to be ready and in the will of my Father. The Father's will shall be done. I got quiet, and the Spirit spoke, "Daughter, the demons you left in your house have always been there. They have made a nest in your home. First there was one, and then two, and then they became three as they multiplied themselves. You could not see them before, but their eyes were always on you—watching your walk with your Father. They waited for an opportune time to live in your home and grow. But do not worry, for where I am taking you, you will learn to fight for your family while the demons are roaming through your home, through and through attacking them."

I quietly sat listening, and again the voice of the Lord spoke. "Daughter! One by one you will defeat them. They are built for war, and so are you. But you will have to take courage and listen carefully to what the Spirit says to you."

"Take note of everything spoken, not missing a message. If you keep the commands of the Lord your God and walk in his ways, then all the people on earth will see that you are called by the name of the Lord, and they will fear you. You are truly blessed. The Lord will grant you abundant prosperity in the fruit of your womb" (Deuteronomy 28:9–11).

"Remember, daughter, to love the Lord with all your heart and all your soul. Fear the Lord your God. Because the Lord is a jealous God, do not test the Lord your God. And remember to do what is right and good in the Lord's sight" (Deuteronomy 6:13–18).

He continued, "This will give you the victory over the enemy." I cried and began an active conversation with the Holy Spirit of my life.

And he stepped in and began with direction. "Daughter," he said, "you will come across a street, the only street you can see, and you will turn there. The street will only allow you to go one way, and it will be to your right. The name of the street is Mercy Street."

"Thank you, Lord! Now I am getting somewhere." And immediately after I thanked the Father, a great storm brewed. The winds were so strong that they broke the blades of the windshield wipers of the car. I could not see a thing. *Oh no!* I thought. *I better stop the car,* when all of a sudden I could hear a loud sound, the sounds of a trumpet blowing in midair. It got louder and louder. I could hardly stand it. I put my hands over my ears, thinking that this might be serious.

"Lord!" I cried. "Why am I hearing war signals of a trumpet?" I tried to peek out the window of the car looking for any sign of the Lord speaking to me signs of Revelation—the end of time—as I began repenting of my sins the whole while. I looked up for any signs from heaven—hail, a huge mountain, a blazing star, a dark sun or moon, a fallen star, four loose angels, or the Lord Almighty himself (Revelation 8:7–13). I knew the trumpet's signal meant to be still silence.

I was scared out of my mind, thinking maybe this is it for me, but as I looked out of the car, I could not see anything. As I waited, I noticed that the trumpet sounds had stopped, and I could then hear sounds of rushing water. The waves were hitting the car and shaking all the tires of the car. I rolled the window down and noticed the road was completely gone. That's right— gone! The car had started to float. *What now?* I thought. *What's going to happen to me now, Lord?*

Then, less than a minute later, I rolled down my window again and there I was in the middle of a sea, floating with water all around me. *Wow!* I thought. Lord! *This is not going so well.* Immediately after I said that, I looked out, and coming at me quickly a huge beast with fire in his mouth straight at me. He was coming and fast. I looked around in the car for something to hit the beast with or throw at him, thinking that I could wound him and he would flee. "Lord!" I screamed. "Help me find something to fight with!"

I heard a voice saying, "If you lay a hand on him, you will remember the struggle and never do it again! Hope of subduing him is false; the mere sight of him is overpowering. No one is fierce enough to rouse him. Be still!" (Job 41:8–10).

"Be still? Lord! Did you say be still? Lord, this is serious. How do I be still when I am getting ready to die, and death is facing me eye to eye, and you don't see any way out."

"Daughter!" the voice spoke quietly. "He can only die by the sword."

I cried, "A sword? Well, Lord, I sure don't have one of those!"

So I tried to start the car, for I did not know what else to do. Then the beast began to heat up the sea, blowing fire from his mouth continually until the whole sea was fiery red hot! Hot! Hot! I was so afraid I could not pray. I began screaming, and the sea got hotter and hotter. The beast blew until the sea began boiling. He turned it into a boiling pot underneath me. I could hear the bubbling sounds of the fiery sea underneath the car.

"Oh, my God!" I cried out. "This thing is going to boil me, I mean, cook me alive!"

"Lord!" I exclaimed. "You said you would never leave me or forsake me, so then why is this thing cooking me, and what does it want?"

I heard the voice of the Lord saying, "He has many names, and you need to know them. He is called the Red Dragon Leviathan, Rehab, and he is even called the Devil.

"What!" I cried. "You have got to be kidding me. I am in the sea with the devil?"

"Lord!" I cried. "You mean to tell me he can swim too?"

"Great!" I cried. "How do I not fear this Lord? I can't swim. He would catch me!"

And the Spirit of the Lord spoke, "How many are your works, O Lord? In wisdom you made them all. The earth is full of your creatures. There is the sea—vast and spacious, teeming with creatures beyond numbers, living things both large and small. There the ships go to and fro and the leviathan that you formed to frolic there. These all look to you to give them their food at the proper time" (Psalms 104: 24–27).

Oh, I get it now! I thought. *Lord! I left my family because we were out of order, so now I will pay and be eaten by the devil? Am I food for him? Tell me, Lord. Will he feed off of my flesh?*

"No, daughter, you do not understand," the Lord answered. "The sea in its boiling rage inhabited by the sea monster symbolizes the fury of human sin." The Lord continued, "Yet it is stirred up by Satan, and only I can quiet and calm the sea."

Then I again heard the voice of the Lord: "I did it yesterday, and I will do it today. Be quiet and still, daughter. Behold! Listen to the voice of the Father."

"But Lord," I cried. "This is not looking good for me right now. This beast is blowing fire at me, and I could die by the fire out of his mouth!"

And the Lord spoke and said, "If you do what is right, will you not be accepted? But if you do not do what is right, sin is crouching at your door. It desires to have you, but you must master it, and you can" (Genesis 4:7).

"Daughter! Remember the beast can only terrorize the human race. His duty is to plague my chosen ones on earth."

"Lord!" I cried. "He is getting closer and closer to me."

And the Lord said, "Do not be afraid!"

Then I looked, and the beast raised up his feet, hitting the back end of the car. He had the feet of a bear and the mouth of a lion. He roared loudly and more loudly at me and began to shake the car.

"Oh no"! I shouted at the beast. "Why are you doing this?"

The beast kicked the back end of the car harder and faster, spinning it around and around. I felt as though I was on a merry-go-round and began throwing up everywhere—all over the car, the front and backseat over and over again. I felt sick, so sick I could hardly move.

The beast began roaring again and the water got hotter. I did not know how much more I would be able to take. I was starting to pass out from the heat, but I knew I needed to try not to faint, so I began blowing the horn of the car for anyone to help me from heaven. I was calling on everyone—the Father, the Son, the Holy Spirit, the angels, and even the saints under the altar.

"Oh God! Somebody help me please!"

I recited Psalms 91:9–12:

> Then no harm will befall you. No disaster will come near your tent, for he will command his angels concerning you to guard you in all your ways. They will lift you up in their hands so that you will not strike your foot against a stone.

TERROR AND FEAR

"Lord!" I cried. "Send me some angels!" So I kept blowing the horn of the car, thinking to put fear in the beast. But this beast had no fear. He was like a raging mad sea creature. He used his head and broke out the back of the car window glass—all of it. I began to close my eyes and not look at him anymore, praying to the Father.

All of a sudden things got quiet—really quiet. I thanked the Father for all he had done for me, acknowledging that he is the Creator of all things. Then I told him that this time I was afraid, and I needed his help.

Then the Spirit spoke, "Open your eyes, daughter. Always keep your eyes open, and do not fear! Can you pull in the leviathan with a fish hook? Or tie down his tongue with a rope? Can you put a cord through his nose or pierce his jaw with a hook?" (Job 41:1–2).

I responded to the Father: "No, Lord, I cannot catch this beast."

Then the Spirit spoke again: "Nothing on earth is his equal—a creature without fear he looks down on all that are haughty—he is king over all that is proud" (Job 41:33-34).

While listening to the Spirit, I started to pass out. I had no more strength—not even enough to listen to the Father. As I fell asleep, I heard the sounds of wings flapping over the car. The wings covered the entire car, even the back window that the beast had broken out. The wings began closing me in so I could not see a thing. I had no understanding of my situation. I just waited, hoping to just fall asleep; but every time I tried to close my eyes, the wings would wake me.

Those wings would flap and flap and flap and not allow me to sleep! "Lord," I cried, "I can do nothing right—I can't even fall asleep on my own, Lord! Just let me sleep."

Then I heard a voice saying, "Daughter! Be strong and courageous. Do not be afraid or terrified because of them, for the Lord your God goes with you. I will never leave you, nor will I forsake you" (Deuteronomy 31:6).

I began to believe the words that were spoken out of the mouth of the Father. I was thinking to myself, *Maybe the wings are the Father waging war with the beast for me.* I did not say a word as long as the wings covered the car. I kept quiet, listening, and the wings were flapping and flapping, and I began to hear the sound of music, loud music. It sounded like a beautiful choir from heaven singing with the most angelic voices I had ever heard. Singing "Worthy is the lamb—you are holy." They never stopped singing, so I began to join in because I could not help myself. I wanted to be a part of that choir and the beauty of it.

Although I could not see anything, I could hear them, and that was enough for me. Just hearing them sing to the Lord overjoyed me.

I cried out to the Lord, "Oh Lord! I want to admit something to you. Lord! I am willing to die if this is in your will. I am not afraid anymore."

As soon as I said that, the wind stopped blowing, the music stopped, and the wings that covered the car all began to disappear. The sea was gone and so was the beast. Everything was dried up as if there had never been a storm or a sea.

"Lord, thank you!" I cried, and I heard a voice saying, "Fear not, for I have redeemed you. I have summoned you by name. You are mine. When you pass through the waters I will be with you, and when you pass through rivers they will not sweep over you. When you walk through the fire, you will not be burned, for I am the Lord your God, the Holy One of Israel, your Savior" (Isaiah 43:1–3).

I thanked the Father until I fell asleep. This time the Father allowed me to do so. Rest is what God gives us in times of trouble. Rest is what the Lord gave me. I found myself waking up the next day lying down in the front seat of the car. I sat up, and as I looked up, there to my right was a place by the name of Mercy Street.

I thought, *Wow! This is the street the Holy Spirit said I would come across, but how did I get here?"* I began thinking, *I don't remember the car moving at all—oh well!*

I thought I was just happy to be there. "So now, what Lord? What do I do?" I asked the Father.

The voice of the Father spoke, "Get out of the car."

So I got out of the car, at least what was left of it, and I began walking. As I was walking, I noticed something. The pavement of the sidewalk started changing colors. It went from jasper to carnelian, matching the sky. I stopped walking and I looked up. All of a sudden, the stars began falling—seven in all. I was frightened and started to run. As I was running, the rain began to fall again faster and faster down on my head. As I tried to get out of the rain, the ground began to shake, and *hard*. I could hardly stand on my two feet and then fell to the ground. As I was getting up again, dust was flying everywhere, as in a desert.

EATING FROM HIS HANDS

Something or someone had placed me in a wilderness.

"My Lord!" I cried out. "Where am I?" Dust was flying all around me. I would try to get up, but I would fall back down. I would try to get up again, but I would fall back down again. I decided to just lie there until I could see and no longer be falling. As I lay there, I looked. On my right was what looked like another beast, this time it was coming up from under the earth on a chamber. His eyes were on me! Looking right at me! I was so dazzled that I could not move. I was speechless at the size of the beast and the size of the horns on the head of that beast.

Although beautiful, this beast was very calm, coming up out of the ground. I did not know what to do. I could not even stand on my own two feet because of the dust storm. I was frightened and unable to scream. I just sat and waited, quietly watching him. I was so threatened by the size of this beast from under the earth that I was speechless. Even though he was huge, he was beautiful, for he had a face of a lamb. That led to confusion for me.

Because of his unique looks, I stared at him, never taking my eyes off him. Yet, as he began to speak to me, the dust from the earth fled, and the ground stopped shaking through his powers. Immediately, as he spoke, I listened. He said, "I have been looking for you."

"Who are you?" I asked, staring at his horns, amazed at the power that came from his mouth and from the horns of his head.

He spoke again, "You were no longer at the edge of the sea!"

I kept my eyes on him, thinking, *How does this beast know me?* Could this be a messenger of Christ? Confusion had overtaken my spirit. So the beast answered me, "I have always known you, watching and waiting to see where you are going at all times. Where *are* you going?" the beast asked.

I looked at him and answered, "I don't know. Wherever my Father takes me—until then I never know where I am going."

After I spoke this to the beast, he began staring at me, putting more fear and anxiety in me, making me extremely uncomfortable—so much that I began to not trust him. I felt the need to get away from him, and quickly. So I spoke, "I must get going."

And the beast answered, "Wait before you go." The beast began to speak, and I noticed that as he spoke, floods of water began drizzling from his mouth, making me unable to understand his words. His language was becoming unclear to me. I could no longer understand what he was saying or what he represented. He looked like a lamb, but what came from his mouth did not quite sound right or make sense to me. So I started to get up and walk away.

"Wait!" the beast said. "Wait! Before you leave, I have something for you." He leaned down and grabbed a stone from the ground, and he turned it into bread.

"Eat," he said. "You look very hungry."

Wow! I thought. *You are from Christ.* I took the bread from the hands of the beast and ate.

The beast spoke again, "Go! You must finish your journey."

I watched as the beast went back down, down to a chamber under the earth. Under the ground he went. I thought, *Wow! That's strange. Where did he come from? And where did he go?*

I began to run because the rain had started again. As I was running, I noticed my flesh was getting weak. I was losing strength and now needed food to feed my flesh. I grew so hungry I could hardly stand up.

"It was almost as if the bread that the beast fed me did something to my flesh, Lord! Why am I so weak?" I asked, and a soft voice spoke. "The spirit is willing but the flesh is weak. Watch out for the lust of the flesh, lust of the eye, and the pride of life."

I began to fight my weak flesh, singing over and over again, speaking loudly, "It is written that man does not live by bread alone, man does not live by bread alone!" (Matthew 4:1–4).

I was feeding my spirit, and finally my flesh calmed down and I had again gained control over my desires. "Thank you, Lord!" I cried. Immediately I looked and saw a rough encircled street light up with bright lights.

I ran down that street and noticed a large sign that read, "Watch out! So that you don't fall!"

I looked up, and again seven stars began to fall. *Oh my,* I thought, *fallen stars and now I am warned not to fall.* Boy was I scared! I looked up to the sky again and all seven stars disappeared.

Oh Lord! Where did those stars fall? Where did they go? As I was running, I noticed on the street were many churches, seven in all. Each had its own name inscribed on the top. They encircled the whole street. The first one, the church to the left, was called the Church of Ephesus. *Huge!* Then another church sat on the side of Ephesus and was called the Church in Smyrna. *Wow!* I thought, *what is this?* I looked, and there on the edge of the street sitting as though on a hill was a church called the Church in Pergamum. *Oh, how beautiful!*

As I looked through the Church of Pergamum, I saw a very small pretty church called the Church of Thyatira. It was *so* beautiful! Next to it was a tiny church called the Church in Sardis. "What is this?" I asked the Lord. "What are you saying to me?" Then I looked farther down to the end of the circle where there were two more churches. I began thinking, *What is the Lord getting ready to do to me, and why churches?*

I kept running and noticed two more churches. And out of all seven churches, of the last two I noticed the one difference of them all—only one had the doors open and then they were closed. It was called the Church in Philadelphia. Next to it, all the way to the end, was the church in Laodicea, so I decided to enter one of the churches. After all, I had nowhere else to go. I had been running and running with no place at which to arrive. I began thanking the Lord because I could not think of a safer place to be than in a church with my sisters and my brothers.

I cried, "Lord, for sure the sisters and brothers will help me to find my way back!"

I felt so relieved that I would be among the members of the body of Christ. "Lord!" I cried again. "What are you saying to me?"

As I said that, I looked up, and coming at me were four strange-looking creatures. I could not make out what they were, but they were running toward me. Rather, they were coming fast right at me. The closer they came, the better I could make them out –they appeared as a lion, an ox, an eagle, and a very strange-looking man. Faster they came. They were all singing, but I could not understand their song.

THE SEVEN CHURCHES

I was almost frightened to death after watching the creatures running toward me, singing as they came. I knew I had no choice but to go into one of the churches. I had to pick one fast—which one? I was clueless. As I ran, the doors of all the churches flew open, as if I needed to pick one soon. I ran to the Church of Ephesus toward the open door. As I entered the church, a voice called out: "I am the one who holds the seven stars in my right hand and walk about in the midst of the churches."

"Lord!" I asked. "Where did the stars go?"

Again the voice spoke, "They are the messengers within the churches, daughter!" The Lord called out: "Remember, I am both her Lord and her judge. I love them all. You must listen to what the Spirit says."

And the Spirit began to speak, "All my children will be under the grace, forgiveness, renewal, guidance, and motivation through the seven-fold presence of the Holy Spirit."

As I entered the church, I noticed that no one greeted me. It was as if I was not there. No one stood at the entrance of the church to give greetings—not one. It was as if I was not there. I began looking around for a seat and wandered toward the front of the church. I noticed an empty seat and began to sit down when a woman grabbed me by the hand. Quickly she said, "Get up! Get up now!"

"Why?" I asked.

"Get up now!" she said. "These seats are only for the overseers and deacons."

I pulled my hand away from her and I said, "I am not moving from this seat," so the woman grabbed me by the hand and took me all the way to the back of the church, and in the corner she sat me down.

"This is where you belong," she said, and she walked away energetic and smiling, not saying another word to me. Everybody in the church looked back at me and began whispering with one another, laughing. I wondered what they were laughing at. I felt so humiliated that I just sat quietly, feeling uninvited and unwanted. Yet I humbled myself by not saying a word as they rolled their eyes, pointing at me. *Wow! This is strange,* I thought.

Then, I heard a voice saying, "For everyone who exalts himself will be humbled, and he who humbles himself will be exalted" (Luke 14:11). Not letting my spirit become angry, I humbled myself. I began looking around the whole sanctuary, and every seat was filled. I thought, *Wow, something is not looking right with these members.* I looked around again. *Wait a minute*! I noticed that all the people in the church looked alike. They all wore the same attire—they all wore a huge helmet on their heads and a matching vest; a belt was wrapped around their waist, and boots covered their feet. *Wow!* I thought. *What is this?*

As I began to get up, the whole church stood up with me and then turned to face me. I could then read what was written on them—on their heads was written *salvation*, on their chest *righteousness*, around their waist *truth*, on their shoes *ready*. And as they stood up, I saw the swords on their sides.

The swords read *word of God* and the blades looked sharp. At that point they all pulled them out on me. "Wait! Wait!" I cried. "I am not here to hurt anyone. Listen, Church, the Father sent me here. Please! Please! Don't hurt me!"

Then the man at the altar stood up and came toward me. "Who are you?" he asked. "You look dark!"

"Dark?" I asked. "What do you mean?"

The man at the altar started to question me: "Did you come from the outside world? Are you here scheming with the devil against our church?"

"No!" I said. "I am a child of God. What are you thinking?" I added, "Sir. I am not a child of the devil!"

The man then said, "This church does not welcome outsiders," and he came at me furiously.

I suddenly grew quiet. My heart was racing over one hundred beats a minute. "Wait a minute," I said. "Listen, Church, listen! Please do not let your self-righteousness judge me!"

Again, everyone began to whisper to one another. "Stop," I cried, "and listen to me. The Lord is love, and not love that is picked out among us. We have to love one another. That means everyone! I am not from darkness. I am from light just like you. We have the same Father!"

Then, the man at the altar spoke. "Who is your Father?"

"Jehovah Shalom (the God of peace)."

The man at the altar spoke again: "Your eyes do not look like ours, which means you are not like us. To me, anyone who does not look like us must be evil, and we can neither be a part of evil nor associate with it."

"Sir"! I said. "You cannot see my light, because your eyes are turned backward inside out—you look at only those you want to see. Those in your clan only…that is a sin against God! You are not walking in love, and that puts you in danger of walking in lawlessness. You are doomed to destruction, and this is sad, because you're refusing to love the truth and be saved. God is truth, and he is love."

I raised my hands in the air, and cried out to the Lord! I began to pray, *what must I do now? There is no love in the eyes of these people. They all looked at me as if they wanted to kill me. Lord, what must I do?*

Then everyone in the church began shouting at once: "Get out!"

"Look!" one woman cried. "She is a Gentile (meaning sinner)."

They all said, "She is not like us. She looks evil," they said. "And she is breaking our law!"

I closed my eyes and began to pray because I saw they were not acting in line with the truth of the Gospel, and it was hurting my heart. I knew that by calling me a Gentile they were calling me a sinner. By saying I was breaking the law, they were saying that they were justifying the law with what they thought was right and good in the eyes of the Lord. *This church was no longer practicing love but lawlessness,* I now was thinking. *Lord, what do I do now?*

When I saw that they were not acting in line with the truth of the Gospel, I said to the man at the altar in front of the whole church, "You are Christians, yet you live like sinners and not like Christians. How is it then that you force sinners to follow Christian customs? How, sir, is that?" (Galatians 2:14).

Then I heard a voice speak: "They are darkened in their "understanding," he said. "and separated from the life of God because of ignorance that is in them due to the hardening of their hearts" (Ephesians 4:18).

So I cried loudly, "Wait, Church, I get it. I know what is wrong here. Don't worry; we can fix this," I said. "The Spirit is speaking to me. If you have any encouragement from being united with Christ, if any comfort from his love, if any fellowship with the Spirit, if any tenderness and compassion, then make my joy complete by being like-minded—having the same love, being one in spirit and purpose. Do nothing out of selfish ambition or vain conceit, but humility. Consider others better than yourselves" (Philippians 2:1–3).

I spoke, "I know you love the Lord, and so do I. for this reason I kneel before the Father from whom his whole family in heaven and on earth derives its name. I pray that out of his glorious riches he may strengthen you with power through his Spirit in your inner being so that Christ may dwell in your hearts through faith, and I pray that you be rooted and established in love, having power together with all saints to grasp how wide and long and high and deep is the love of Christ" (Ephesians 3:14–18).

After I spoke, the man at the altar said, "Lady! Did you just say that we should consider you better than us? Lady, you are crazy. Not only do you come from the outside of the dark world, but you also now are claiming to be a teacher of Christ?"

I looked up, and they all began chasing me. A little girl to my right threw me a sword. She said, "You will need this," and I began to fight one by one as they were fighting me. I could tell they had no problem fighting anyone who did not look like them, and they did not fight fair. One by one, they fought me.

I was determined I was not giving up, so I fought back to show them I was suited up. That I was not quitting also made them angry. What a burden I was carrying—and a heavy burden! *Here I am in a church, and I have to fight my own sisters and brothers. We are fighting over the same God—the God of the heavens and the God of our salvation.* That weighed heavy on my soul because the Lord Jesus Christ said to love one another, and it was concerning me that these were the meanest church people I had ever known. Still, I was determined not to quit fighting.

Finally, a woman in the church came from the back, and she grabbed me by the hair. "Oh! Do you think you can fight?" she said. "Do you think you are not going to give up?"

I looked up at her and I shouted, "No! I will not give up!"

So the woman picked me up. My Lord, was she strong, carrying me across her back. Then she threw me out the front doors of the church, flat on my face. I landed hard and just lay there looking up to the heavens, wondering, *How can anyone claim to love you, Lord, and treat his brothers and sisters like that?*

The entire law is summed up in a single command: "Love one another," (John 15:17) but they were all bound to each other.

I cried to the Lord and heard a voice saying, "I have said, love your neighbor as yourself. If you keep on biting and devouring each other, watch out! Or you will be destroyed by each other" (Galatians 5:14–15).

So as I lay there on the ground crying, I began to see a shadow—a large shadow—lingering over my face. I was afraid to roll over to look. I thought, *Oh no, Lord! Not the demons again!*

"Get up! Get up now!" Screams were coming from the shadows.

"Stand on your feet fitted with readiness of peace, and as a testimony against them, and get going!" I looked over, and it was the ox speaking—the same ox that was chasing me into the churches.

The ox spoke again, "Think! Don't you remember I am a burden carrier? I will carry all your burdens. Jump on my back," he said. "Do not worry!"

So I got up, jumped on the ox's back, and on to the next church we went. As I rode, the ox spoke to me, quieting my spirit. He said, "In the beginning was the word, and the word was with God, and the word was God. He was with God in the beginning" (John 1:1–2).

Then he stopped speaking for a minute, pausing for about seven seconds. Soon he spoke again, "If people do not welcome you, shake the dust off your feet when you leave their town as a testimony against them" (Luke 9:5).

I kept on going, and as I was heading to the next church, I saw the stars falling again—seven of them all falling together. *Wow!* I thought where they were going and why they kept falling from the sky.

And a voice spoke, "The mystery of the seven stars that you see is the messengers for the churches, and (the angels of the seven churches) go ahead of you to give out of my right hand mercy upon the saints" (Revelation 1:20).

Then the ox began to drop me down in front of a church, and into the Church of Smyrna I went. This time I was welcomed—they all welcomed me. "Welcome, sister!" the members said. "Come on in!" They all were laughing and filled with joy, even though they looked to have nothing—no piano, no band, and no music.

I MUST MOVE ON

They only used their hands for clapping, but finally I smiled because of the welcoming joy on their faces. I sat through the service, clapping and enjoying the man at the altar speaking and teaching. He was speaking on God's goodness and grace.

Soon I could see tears welling in everyone's eyes. "Why are you crying?" I asked the members. No one answered me.

"What's wrong?" I asked. No one said a word. I looked into their faces, and I noticed they all looked as if they had not eaten for days. They were all dirty and bruised as if they had been beaten and dragged through dirt and mud over and over again.

I began looking around the whole church, and they all looked the same—even the children. *Oh my*! I thought. "What is wrong, Church? Why the sadness? I asked. Are you all in danger of your lives?"

No one spoke. "What has happened to you?" Again, no one spoke. I asked emphatically, "What happened to you? How long have you all been suffering violence? And by whom?"

"Look at me!" I shouted. "Who is beating you all up?"

Immediately, all the members began to cry again, even the man at the altar. They all started to sing once more, giving praises to the Lord.

"Stop! Talk to me," I said. "Do not fear. Let me help you. Don't you know to fear anything besides God? Is it a sin and can it endanger your faith?"

"Trust God!" I pleaded.

"Get up," I cried. "Let's all get out of here!" It looked like all the members were afraid to move.

Finally, the man at the altar spoke. He said, "We can't go with you."

"Why?" I asked.

"The devil is outside roaming, and we are afraid."

"Don't be afraid," I answered. "We should be faithful to the point of death."

"No!" the man at the altar said. "We will just sit here for ten days and wait."

"Ten days?" I asked. "What do you mean?"

"Ten days means God has put a time on our persecution, so we will just wait upon the Lord. He decides for us how long we must suffer." The man then said to me, "Now, sister, you better go! Because in a half hour the devil will be back and enter the church, and he will beat you as well."

"What!" I exclaimed. "You mean to tell me that the devil comes into your church to beat you up, and your members?"

"Yes," the man at the altar said.

And I asked him, "Then why do you let him beat you and all your members up? You should be setting an example for the church!"

The man just looked at me and said, "We have no choice. We fear things would begin to get worse for us, and they do. At least we know he is coming, and accept that he is coming."

He then spoke and told me that the Father would stop him when he is ready—meanwhile they should rejoice and be glad.

"Yes," I said to the man at the altar. "Rejoice and be glad, but you are making an idol of the devil. You are bowing down to him in fear. Your fear is worshiping the enemy."

"Please," I cried, "don't fear anything but God. He is a jealous God."

"Yes," I cried. "We sometimes are persecuted, but we do not let Satan come in to torment us. We fight during our time of trouble and persecution, not by setting up a temple table for the enemy. Do you not know? Satan is a liar; he will tell you all kinds of discouraging words during this time to try to lessen your faith in the Father."

"Please, sir. Be careful during these times. The enemy will shred you to pieces under these conditions. Don't sit here and wait on his lies."

"Get up!" I shouted. "Let's get out of here!"

As I was speaking, I heard a voice say, "The knowledge of the secrets of the kingdom of God has been given to you. But to others I speak in parables so that though seeing, they may not see; though hearing, they may not understand. The seed is the word of God. Those along the path are the ones who hear, and then the devil comes and takes away the word from their hearts so that they may not believe" (Luke 8:10–12).

The man at the altar looked at me. He spoke, "Bless you, but no! You go run! Get out of here because the Word says, 'Blessed is the man who perseveres under trial because when he has stood the test he will receive the crown of life that God has promised to those who love him'" (James 1:12).

The man looked at me and spoke, "You had better run while you are still strong. Go so he doesn't beat you up too."

I began to stand up because after hearing this, I needed to be on my feet ready to run yet ready to fight. I was saddened for them, really saddened. I wanted to stay with them, for although they served God, all their fear was in the devil and not God giving them lack of knowledge, unable to see, hear, or understand the Father. Although they were facing death daily, they were holding on—but holding on in fear because they knew that Christ knew about their pain and the condition of bondage that they were suffering. This made them rich, yet in poverty.

The man spoke, "Go, woman! Leave so we put no stumbling block in anyone's path so that our ministry will not be discredited. Rather, as servants of God, we command ourselves in every way in great endurance in troubles, hardship and distresses, in beatings, in imprisonment, riots, in hard work, sleepless nights and hunger, in purity, understanding, patience and kindness—in the Holy Spirit and in sincere love."

The man then said, in truthful speech and in the power of God, "With the weapons of righteousness we will persevere" (2 Corinthians 6:3–7). We thank you for your concerns, but you better leave, because this may be too dangerous for you, and we will accept our situation no other way."

The man then said, "Sister, look at me," and I looked at him with tears in my eyes.

"He said, "We will overcome this. We may be hurt by the first death (which is physical), but the second death (which is spiritual) will not hurt us at all."

As I left, these words made me cry, but then I noticed that as I was walking out and looked down, all the members of the church were chained to their seats, even the children. It was that Satan had already chained them down. He was coming into the church and beating them all up.

My heart was beating fast. Again I was thinking, *oh my Lord! I don't want to be chained to my seat. Please, Lord!*

And while I was thinking and praying, I heard a voice say, "Lack of faith for any Christian—God's chosen ones—open the doors for this sin if they have left their first love. Fear then follows because the heart no longer looks for the love of God and Christ but other things. The love of God tells them not to be afraid. God will overcome for them."

Then the voice spoke, "Look around at how they have imprisoned themselves."

I began to look around, and I noticed out of the glass of the church were prison bars. *Wow! I have to get out of here; all these people are in prison!* I started to walk out, and as I did, I looked back.

All the members were looking at me and saying, "May God bless you so you can stay strong."

I thought to myself, *Lord, there is something about being imprisoned which humbles a man's heart. These were the most humble people I had ever seen—they were welcoming their suffering instead of avoiding it. They had forgotten that it is during these times that the Father gives favor and rewards for persecution. All they had to do was speak to the fear, and it would flee, yet the enemy was their fear—it had taken their courage to fight. They all were just sitting and waiting for their suffering to be over.*

I decided to leave them waiting, and out of the doors I went. As I was going out, I said, "Lord, have mercy on them."

And I heard a voice saying, "I tell you the devil will put some of you in prison to test you, and you will suffer persecution for ten days. Be faithful even to the point of death, and I will give you the crown of life" (Revelation 2:10).

"I am he who is the first and the last."

I started to run. I did not know what to expect, and as I fled, I saw a lion coming at me fast and roaring and as powerful as ever. "Oh no"! I cried. I picked up a stick from the ground and yelled, "Get back! Get back!" I yelled to the lion's face.

And he spoke, saying, "I can catch you if I want to, and quickly because I am powerful."

I ran even faster to get into the next church.

THE DONKEY DID IT

Finally I made it to the Church of Pergamum, and I noticed that outside of the church was a donkey tied to a tree with a strange look on his face. So I stopped and walked close up to him, and he gave me eye-to-eye contact. I noticed the donkey had duct tape on his mouth. *What is this all about?* I thought. I was afraid to remove the tape, so I gazed at him and asked who had put this tape on his mouth? The donkey was looking straight at the Church of Pergamum. His eyes got bigger and bigger, which made me curious about what the donkey was trying to say to me, so I decided to remove the tape from the donkey's mouth. When I did, he began to sneeze.

"Bless you," I said to him.

The donkey answered, "No, sister. May the creator of the heavens, earth, and sea bless you. You will need it."

The donkey began speaking louder and louder saying to the angels of the Church in Pergamum to listen. Carefully he said, "This church shall be judged by him who has the sharp doubled-edged sword. Satan roamed to and fro of this church, and you have all chosen to look the other way."

The donkey then said to me, "Watch out! For he and his disciples do not look the other way."

"Oh no, Lord!" I cried. "I don't want to go into that church!" After I cried out to the Lord, immediately the lion showed up and again ran toward me, this time with fire in his eyes. I cried, "Look!" Pointing at the lion, I began picking up sticks from the ground to fight with.

The donkey began singing, watching me singing, and singing. "Shut up! Shut up! Right now!"

I cried out at the donkey, "Don't you see that lion is coming, and he is going to eat us alive?"

But the donkey kept singing on and on, babbling and babbling and babbling over and over again. He sang, "One, two, three, Satan is looking at me. Four, five, six, you better drop those sticks. Seven and eight, keep your eyes straight. Nine and ten is where the fighting begins."

After hearing the donkey sing, I was so scared that I forced the duct tape back on his mouth to shut him up and ran as fast as I could into the Church of Pergamum. I entered through the back doors. I was so scared and not wanting the members to think that the donkey sent me through the front doors. As I entered, I noticed in church everybody seemed happy. They were all singing and clapping their hands to the music, and welcomed me.

"Come, sister," the ladies said. "Sit down," and I did.

I was seated in the front of the church. *Wow!* I thought. *How nice.* I was thinking that this church was so beautiful and looked rich everywhere. Everybody was clothed nicely, and they were all wearing silver and gold jewels. I looked up, and the man at the altar was standing beside the offering bowl—the biggest offering bowl I had ever seen. The bowl was huge and all covered in gold and silver. I looked, and next to the man at the altar was another man who was also standing. He was looking around, making sure that no one got close to that bowl. This bowl was beautiful. It was displayed in front of the church for everyone to see. I watched as the music stopped, and the man at the altar spoke.

"Church!" he said. "We are in need, and I will need everyone to give all that they have."

Wow! I thought. *I don't have any money.*

"Church"! the man cried. "Stand up and open your Bible, and let's read."

I looked to my side and grabbed a Bible and I opened it. *Wow! What is this?* Every page of the Bible was torn out except the book of Malachi, and then the man at the altar said, "Church, stand for the reading of the word, and we all stood up. He spoke, "Will a man rob God?"

And the whole church said, "No!"

Then the man at the altar said, "But you asked, how do we rob you?"

Then the whole church said, "In tithes and offering," and the man at the altar, alone with the men around the bowl all began to laugh loudly. *Wow!* I thought. *I wonder what's so funny to them.* I began to look around, and I noticed all the members had stamps on their foreheads. One would read *wicked*, and one would read *righteous*. I looked again at the man at the altar, and he had two stamps on his head, which read *wickedly righteous*, and he just kept on laughing, as the members placed their offerings into the bowl.

He did not care what was given nor did he not care if their forehead stamp read *wicked* or *righteous*. "Bring everything to me," he kept saying. "Everything you got!" laughing the whole while.

Oh God! I thought. *He's making me sick with his laugh.*

"Make him stop!" I cried to the Lord. The man got louder and louder with his laugh. I stood up, and I yelled, "Stop laughing! Sir, you are making me sick." The whole church sat down except the man at the altar.

"What's so funny to you?" I asked the man at the altar, and he began looking at me with his huge black eyes.

He said loudly, "Did you give?"

I said to the man at the altar, "Yes, I have given to God. I have not robbed God. How have I not robbed him? I have turned from my wicked ways. I have given the gift of holiness, and holiness is what God desires with repentance."

"Repentance!" the man shouted. "God needs you to bring to the storehouse!"

I began walking toward the man at the altar, and I said, "Yes, he does. Yes, God wants us to give to the storehouse bringing him tithes and offerings, sir. As a matter of fact, since you are still standing on the old Mosaic law (corban) and not the New Testament law, your teachings are still wrong. We are New Testament Christians now, and there is no need for sacrifice for sin. The Father did it once, and for all for us" (Hebrews 10:11–18).

I looked at the man of the altar, and he was no longer laughing. I knew I had to have spoken with truth and with boldness because the truth will wipe the smile off anyone's face, and the man did not like what I was saying.

So I said, "Sir, you see the Father now wants us to draw near to him. He wants a new offering corban (that is a gift devoted to God)" (Mark 7:11).

"God determines what is pleasing to him, so we should give to the Father what is pleasing to him. We should give to the Father the gift of our life, for he wants our love commitment and services" (Deuteronomy 6:5).

"There is no more need for blood to be shed. Jesus Christ, our Savior did it all for us. We are no longer to practice this religious duty again and again, offering the same sacrifices which can never take away our sins (Hebrews 10:11), so the tenth that you collect is a sacrifice for a guilt offering—guilt of sins, which can never take away our sins."

"For this reason, Jesus Christ our Lord and Savior did a one-time sacrifice for all once and for all so we would no longer have to pay."

I continued, "Sir, this is what our Father wants. He wants holiness in this house, he wants the whole entire house to be holy, and to serve him, and there, and then will he accept your offerings, and your choice gifts alone with your holy sacrifices" (Ezekiel 20:40–41).

I said, "But you seem to be enjoying this as if this is all for you. Is the money all for you?"

The man at the altar began to walk close up to me and said, "What did you say?"

I looked at the man eye to eye, and I replied, "You read Malachi, but you don't understand, because your eyes are closed."

"Tell me, woman," he shouted. "What do you think Malachi means?"

I said, "Sir, the prophet Malachi was sent by God. Malachi means (my messenger) my angel, the last prophet sent by God to give Israel one last chance. He was sent from heaven to speak to Israel known as a burden of the word of the Lord. Sir, you need to repent, because what you are doing is wrong, and unlike so many, you should not peddle the word of God for profit."

I told the man at the altar, "If Malachi is all you read, then the love of money is who you are serving if nothing else matters to you in the whole Bible but Malachi. Then you have become selfish, and the money is all about you."

"Go on!" the man said.

Then I spoke again. I said, "Yes, God made admonition with you a covenant of blessings just as was given to the Levites to collect for the work of the ministry. Yes, you deserve a gift," I said. "Yet God has this against you. You have become greedy and wicked. You have received many offerings, offerings from the wicked, offerings that are lame, blind, sick, and torn."

"Your gifts are unacceptable to God. Your men have traded their godly wives for ungodly wives, wives that are filled with evil and perversion, causing the men to mistreat the wives of their youth, women who have stood by them when they were weak, and now that they are strong, you are allowing them to divorce, and trade for women who do not even know the God that we serve causes ungodly offspring."

"But behold! This is what God has to say about you. You expected much but see it turned out that what you brought home was little. I blew it away."

"Why?" asks the Lord Almighty. "Because of my house, which remains ruined, while each of you is busy with his own house; therefore, because of you the heavens have withhold their dew, and the earth its crops. I called for a drought on the fields, and mountains on the grain, the new wine, the oil, and whatever the ground produces on men and cattle, and on the labor of your hands. This is a call to build the house of the Lord" (Haggai 1:9–11).

"You have filled the altar with tears to the Lord. No one can serve two masters .Either he will hate the one and love the other, or he will be devoted to the one and despise the other. You cannot serve both God and Money. (Matthew 6:24). I looked at him closely and said, "You are compromising your doctrine finances, marriage, honesty, and morals in this church. You see deception in the house of the Lord, but yet! You turn a deaf ear to it."

I continued, "Because of the love of money, do you not see a blind sacrifice meaning the man's heart is not into giving? A sick sacrifice means that a man did not work for the kingdom of God to earn this sacrifice. A lame sacrifice means a man's thoughts are vain, and a torn sacrifice means evil givens. You see, sir, what you are receiving God doesn't want. You are mocking God. You bring a curse upon yourself and should teach your members better, because God has taught you better."

After I said this, he said, "Really!"

I said, "Sir, you had better believe, really."

Then the man said, "Church, watch this!" The man at the altar raised up his feet, jumped in the air, and kicked me in the head, knocking me out cold.

I woke up tied to the altar with duct tape on my mouth as the donkey had been out back, tied up, with everybody laughing at me; dizzy and glazed. I called out to the Lord, "Lord! Help me, help me, Lord! Please."

And I heard a voice speak, and now! The voice said, "This admonition is for you, oh priest. If you do not listen, and if you do not set your heart to honor my name, says the Lord Almighty, he will send a curse upon you, and he will curse your blessings. Yes, I have already cursed them, because you have not set your heart to honor me. Because of you, I will rebuke your descendants. I will spread on your faces the offal from your festival sacrifices, and you will be carried off with it. And you will know that I have sent you this admonition so that my covenant with Levites may continue, says the Lord Almighty" (Malachi 2:1–4).

I looked, and I noticed some of the members that had the stamp of *righteous* stood beside me to remove the duct tape from my mouth, and they began to pray with me. They said, "Lord! There is a Nicolaitan spirit in our church, and the body of Christ accepts it."

They began crying out for the body, asking for forgiveness and deliverance in the church, and they cried, "Lord! This spirit is dangerous."

This spirit teaches them that they made Christianity conform to the world instead of Christianity changing the world, and it was accepted here in the body of

Christ. They began to cry and cry with their hearts saddened and their faces downcast.

Hearing them, the man at the altar approached me. He whispered in my ear as they were praying and said, "Lady, did you not see that donkey outside?"

He also would not shut up and was babbling and babbling on and on about the things he did not know, and then he began walking away.

"My thoughts were with the Lord," I confirmed. "Lord, have mercy upon this church that is being led by a fighting man at the altar leading the house of the Lord. Lord, this church needs you."

"Please untie me," I cried out, "because I remember the donkey warnings saying to me, 'Watch out for the devil and his disciples!'" As I was crying, I could still hear the prayers of the righteous in that church. I continued to cry out, "Let me go!"

And then those who feared the Lord talked with each other and said, "Let her go! Untie her! Free her from this bondage, these chains that are weighing her down." Immediately afterward in came the lion into the church, roaring loudly, with sounds of thunder breaking out all the glass and windows of the church, heading straight to the altar where I stood.

"Help! Help!" I cried. Nobody was around, and it was as if they all disappeared. It was just me and the lion, and I was in fear and trembling. I watched as he came up to me, looking at me with fire in his eyes. As I gazed at him, he dropped a tear on the side of my face, and that gave me strength.

LEAVING THE DWELLING PLACE OF SATAN

After the tears fell, the lion opened his mouth and roared with power. All the chains from my body fell off so that I was freed, and out the door I ran, never looking back. By this time, I thought to myself I have had enough. I wanted to find that old car, get in it, and go home.

Then I heard a voice speak. "Repent!" he said. "Therefore, otherwise, I will soon come to you and will fight against them with the sword of my mouth" (Revelation 2:16).

So I began to head toward the next church, and as I was running, a hailstorm came. Frightened, without anything to cover my head, I began to pray. "Lord," I cried. "Cover me. Cover me, Lord!" Immediately, a shadow of light came over my head covering my whole body and stayed with me as I kept on running and the hail kept coming. I was feeling the climax of God's divine wrath in his anger over the sins and rebellion of mankind. I cried for the churches because I knew that the force of hail was to show us God's power, and that his name might be proclaimed in all the earth. There is no one like God. (Exodus 9:13–28).

I began to look for a place of shelter, and quickly, so I looked up and I saw another church. This church was huge. It was dome-shaped with windows at least one hundred feet high. As I ran up the steps to go through the large opened doors, the doors closed on me without letting me in. I thought, *How do I get in now, Lord?* By that time, the hailstorm was in full progress.

I ran on the side of the church, and I found an opened window, and into the Church of Thyatira I went, soaked and wet. Through the window I went and ended up behind some long, beautiful, purple silk curtains. Behind the curtains was an exquisite baptism pool with water the color of the sky, and there I talked with the Lord: "Lord, I want this. I want to be in this pool." So I stood behind the curtains just looking at the water in the baptism pool and thanking God for the blood of the lamb, the water, and the baptism.

As I waited there, a woman entered through the door. "Hello," she said. I jumped up, frightened by her voice. "Welcome to the Church of Thyatira!" My eyes were amazed at how beautiful she was, yet very soft spoken.

"What is your name?" she asked. I told her that I could not remember my name.

"Sure you do," she replied. "Your Father renamed you, and he now calls you Beautiful."

"Beautiful. How do you know that?" I asked.

Then the woman said, "Because my name is Jezzie, and the Spirit speaks to me. It tells me all things you mean you are."

"A prophetess?" I asked.

The woman grabbed me by the hand and said, "Come, let me tell you some things." She sat me down by the baptism pool and she said, "I know all that you have been through. You are struggling with many things."

She continued, "You are on a forbidden journey—a journey that has been caused by the law of your sins." She began to tell me everything I had been through in my past, things that was so painful I did not even remember them. She reminded me of everything about my life, placing such a burden so heavy on my shoulders that I began to weep.

She grabbed me as I began to faint, and the she said, "Be strong, Beautiful, and don't worry, for I can help you. I know the reason for this pain!" She said, "Look down!"

"Where?" I asked Jezzie.

She said, "Look down into the water." I looked down, and as I was looking I noticed the Ten Commandments were encrypted at the bottom of the pool. "You cannot possibly keep all these commandments now, can you?" the woman asked me.

I don't know. Is there danger in the water?

She knew exactly what I was thinking. She had me puzzled, and she answered what I had in mind. "Yes, this was the very reason Eve sinned. She was given a law—a commandment—something impossible for her to keep." Jezzie continued, "Eve could not keep the law, and nor will you."

Then she looked at me and she said, "But guess what? I have the solution for this forbidden journey that you are on. It has helped many of the members at this church. I helped them also and I can help you, and it's only because I speak what the Spirit says. I am going to help you to get back were you come from."

Wow! I thought to myself. *All I want is to get back home.* "Okay, I like that!"

I told the woman to keep talking, and she said, "And when you are going back, you will not even need that old car again, because the man at the altar will take you in his helicopter and fly you back home!"

Wow! "Let's go. Let's go!" I cried.

Jezzie said, "Wait a minute. Calm down. Just one more thing, and listen to me closely. You will need to do *one* more thing."

"What! What! Tell me," I cried, "and I will do it."

She said, "Beautiful, just remember this water will lead you astray, so forget about it. Forget about the baptism. It knows that man cannot live by the laws of it." She added, "That is why immediately after the baptism of Jesus he was led to be tempted by the devil (Matthew 4:1). Who can stand up to temptation but Christ?"

Speaking quietly, she said, "Not us. That is why one can be baptized one day and begin to sin the next. It's a setup! You cannot possibly live up to the law if you try, Beautiful. You will be back."

I said, "Wait a minute, Jezzie, are you telling me that I should deny my Christ and the baptism, and by doing this my forbidden journey will end, and I will not have to fight the creatures in my home? What about my family? They don't see them, but I do. And the creatures will destroy them all, and I will still have a demon's nest set up in my home fighting against my family in everything they do."

I looked at the woman and I said, "Jezzie, I want them gone and away from my family and me. I love my family, and I love my Christ. I want my family all baptized with the Holy Spirit. I want them saved, and I want the enemy out of my house."

I began telling Jezzie all of my family secrets, and when I finished, she looked at me and said, "Beautiful, I have been a member of this church for a long time, and I know the truth. No one can live a life without sin. Sin is why you are here."

Then she looked at me, and she questioned me: "Did God really say you had to follow this journey? And that you could not go back?"

I tried to remember, and finally I answered her, "No, Jezzie, the Lord did not say that, but he did say, 'Daughter, you will go wherever I take you.'"

She said, "See, Beautiful? Well then, don't worry. If it was not for your corrupt nature and for the law, you would not be on this forbidden path. If you continue on this path, you will live your life with thorns, thistles, and pain, and then the ultimate death in the world."

"Oh no, Jezzie! I don't want to die."

She replied, "Beautiful, you cannot live without sin. I can teach you a secret about the wages of sin. This secret will show you how to live with them." It was almost as if she had already known what was going on in my home. It was as though she knew about the creatures, and that they were there fighting my family and waiting on me. She even knew there were more than one.

She called out the spirits as *them,* meaning many, so then Jezzie began telling me everything I wanted to hear, which gave me a feel-good effect at that time, motivating me again, telling me exactly what I wanted to hear, taking my mind off everything I had been going through. Oh my! Did this prophetess make me feel good at that time!

So I asked, "Jezzie, how did you know all these things about me?"

I began to wonder how she knew me, and she said, "Beautiful, because I have secrets."

"What secrets? Tell me, Jezzie, what secrets?"

She said, "I have secrets that will take you back from the beginning, and I know a shortcut back for you. Come closer to me and let me tell you."

I came close to her and placed my ears up to her mouth, and the woman whispered softly into my ears.

"What are you saying, Jezzie? I cannot hear you!"

She whispered again. "Louder!" I cried. "Tell me, for I cannot hear you," and the woman let out a scream that sounded like it came from the pits of hell.

It was so loud that I passed out, and when I woke up, I found myself looking down, hovering over my own body. *Oh no! What is this?* I thought. *How did I get up here? And with my body down there!* I was in front of the altar of the church lying in a casket with people standing around me as though it was a funeral and I was the guest of honor.

"Oh, my God"! I cried. "You mean to tell me that Jezzie is a church witch and a false prophet? Not only did she lead me astray, but she also deceived me. She is

attractive and talented but indeed wicked and unright-
eous, yet understanding of the law of God. I cannot
believe this. I let that woman put me in a grave by ton-
ing down the faith I had in Christ Jesus, weighing me
down with things that my Christ has already brought
me through now."

"What, Lord?" I cried. "How do I get out of this
mess? And where is the man at the altar? Where is he
in all of this sin? Jezzie promised me he would fly me
home in his helicopter. It seemed that he had flown
himself home and left his members in the hands of
this woman."

I began to pray. "Lord, help me. I cannot move a
muscle in my body." Everything on my body was stiff
and numb like a cork. I could see and cry out to the
members, yet they could not hear me.

I looked to the left of the altar, and there was Jezzie.
She was laughing and talking to other members of the
church. "I am going to get you, Jezzie!" I threatened.
"You demonic spirit"! Lord, get her! Get her, please,
now! Please, Lord, don't let her get away with this."
I could not believe what I was seeing. There she was,
standing by the grave that she had placed me in.

She was laughing and talking, and all the members
of the church were around her, smiling and enjoying
her beauty. I cried out to her, "Repent, Jezzie! Repent!"

She began to speak to me without moving her
mouth. "No!" she cried. "I will not repent."

"You are refusing to repent and are constantly
spreading your poison throughout the church!" I kept
screaming and hoping someone would hear me. "Eloem

is going to get you, Jezzie. He is going to come down and wipe that smile from your face because of the spirit in you. You carry around death, and it has caused you to be deceptive, manipulative, dominant, viciously scheming, and wicked."

She only laughed louder. "You are the devil!" I yelled. "As a matter of fact, Jezzie, death shall be yours. Your grave sin will catch up with you. I promise one day the Father will cast you on your bed of suffering" (Revelation 2:21–23).

"Keep laughing if you think this is funny!" I cried out to the church, "Watch out! Watch out, people!"

Immediately Jezzie began to lower her lips to my ear again. "Get away from me!" I shouted. "Get away from me, Death," I cried. "Stop her, Lord. What is she about to do to me now?"

As I was crying, she began to kiss me on the cheek.

"Oh no! You did not just kiss me. Oh, how evil," I cried. "Lord! Will you give me the strength to raise up my hand just once and strike off her ear?"

Jezzie laughed and lowered her face down to mine, and then she whispered to me, "Because I find this law at work: When I want to do good, evil is right there with me, for in my inner being I delight in God's law. But I see another law at work in the members of my body. Waging war against the law of my mind and making me a prisoner of the law of sin at work within my members. What a wretched man I am. Who will rescue me from this body of death?" (Romans 7: 21-24)

"My Lord!" I cried. "This is one wicked woman— and one corrupt church to see the things she does and say nothing. Death is what she brings," I shouted. "My Lord, where are those destroying angels when you need them? I could surely use one or two right about now!"

I thought, *Lord, look at what she did to me.* I cried, "Lord, did you just hear what she said to me? That she is wretched and deadly! Abba, help me. Evil is all around me. It's what she is at her best; she calls herself a prophetess, yet she is a witch. How will I get home now?"

After I said that, Jezzie looked at me lying still, and she said, "It is too late for you now," and then she pointed to a door in the church that read *deep*.

Oh, I get it now. The secret was my bed of suffering and not hers. She made me pay for her sins, and I felt that it was over for me now. She had me bound and lying in a casket. She talked and I listened, and I died. I was beginning to accept it, and the men in the church began pushing me through the doors that she pointed to.

As I was going in through the doors, I cried, "Well, Lord, it's over now. I accepted the prophetess' wisdom. Now death is mine."

As I went through the doors, I looked at the room ahead which was filled with the dead bodies of the members of the church. I looked again. *What is this? Oh my Lord!* I thought. Look at all these people she has destroyed.

Whole families—even the children—she put in graves. *Oh great!* I thought. *She does this a lot.*

"Lord," I cried. "You said, 'Watch out for the false prophets. They will come to you in sheep's clothing, but inwardly they are like ferocious wolves'" (Matthew 7:15).

"Well, Lord! It's true, and she was a beautiful wolf looking like an angel of light."

And a voice spoke to me. It said, "For such men are false apostles. Deceitful workmen are masquerading as apostles of Christ and no wonder. For Satan himself masquerades as an angel of light, and it is not surprising if his servants masquerade as servants of righteousness. Their end will be what their actions deserve" (2 Corinthians 11:13–15).

After hearing this from the Father, I began to grieve. "Lord, help me!"

I could not hear him anymore. It was as if the Lord was no longer listening or speaking to me.

"Please, Lord! Don't be angry with me. Please, Lord! Forgive me of my sin of unfaithfulness. Please, Lord!"

And then I could hear a voice speak. It said, "Remember the *watch out*! This was the one of the watch-outs for those who will deceive you and leave you for dead, with all kinds of false prophets weighing you down with false hope."

The voice then said, "But yet, the Lord your God will never leave you or forsake you, for the Lord is your helper."

I began to cry because I felt that I was so unworthy of the Lord's forgiveness, and I felt that I did not deserve that he should give me another chance. I felt saddened by this because I knew better to fall for those lies. *My God, where was my faith in that darkness?* I was only looking at me and what I wanted rather than what God wanted of me.

LORD, PLEASE GIVE ME ONE MORE CHANCE

I closed my eyes and I said, "Lord, I have sinned against you, and it has caused my death. I did not do what was righteous."

And the voice said, "But now righteousness from God apart from law has been made known to which the law and prophets testify. This righteousness from God comes through faith in Jesus Christ to all who believe. There is no difference, for all have sinned and fall short of the glory, and are justified freely by his grace through the redemption that came by Christ Jesus. He did this to demonstrate his justice" (Romans 3: 21–26).

I lay quietly, listening, and again the Spirit questioned me: "Do you believe?"

I said, "Yes, I believe."

And the voice answered, "And without faith it is impossible to please God, because anyone who comes to him must believe that he exists and that he rewards those who earnestly seek him" (Hebrews 11:6). And then the Lord raised me up out of my grave, and I climbed out of that casket, and throughout the church

I ran, passing everybody in the church and not looking back. Out the doors I ran, filled with joy.

I cried out for those in the church, and as I was praying for them, praying for each and every one of them, I thought, *Lord, they seemed so prosperous and very beautiful—flying around in a church helicopter, fancy attire, beautiful women, and golden altars.*

Tears began rolling down my face. I could hear these words: "Many live as enemies of the cross of Christ, and their destiny is destruction. Their God is their stomach, and their glory is in their shame. Their mind is on earthly things, but our citizenship is in heaven, and we eagerly await a savior from there, the Lord Jesus Christ" (Philippians 3:18–20).

And the Spirit said, "Now I say to the rest of you in Thyatira, to you who do not hold to her teaching and have not learned Satan's so-called deep secrets. I will not impose any other burden on you. Only hold on to what you have until I come" (Revelation 2:24–25).

I said, "Thank you, Lord. It is still not too late for them." And out the doors I went, thanking God that he did not leave me for dead in that church, and that I was given another chance to live again. After this, I was determined nothing would get in my way; and as I was running down the street to the next church, an eagle flew over me and hovered over my body. I could feel his presence all over me. It felt so warm around me, and I felt as if there was no need to even look up. Oh, how the eagle blessed me as I was running. He gave me strength to go on, warming my body from the coldness of death. As he spread his wings over my body, he began to sing me the most beautiful song I had ever heard: "You are holy, Lord God Almighty. Worthy is the lamb."

"Oh, my God," I cried. "You are worthy," and the eagle never stopped singing and bringing me joy with his presence. So I began to thank the Father for the morning star (the Holy Spirit) that cares for the angels for the sake of his saints. I was thinking, *Lord, you give Jesus, the morning star, to judge, to separate the sheep from goats with your staff.* I continued to thank him because it was then that I understood why I could not enter through the front doors of that church.

I had been warned that judgment was theirs. I was in desperate need of the strength of the Father. I felt drained just being in the presence of that church, yet I thanked God that I shared the authority with Christ. It would give me the strength to go forward and to break free and rise from the dead back to the living. It had given me life instead of death. I had much to be grateful for. I prayed, thanking God that because of Jezzie I was able to see that *Jezebel* was a spirit there at the church—a quiet whispering spirit, a church secret.

So as I was thanking my Father for her because of the death she brought to me, my faith was questioned, and it was by my faith that I was able to rise up again with warmness. It was given to me by the Father. I shouted out to my Lord, "What a beautiful feeling you have given me!"

The eagle began speaking and he said, "So if you think you are standing firm, be careful that you do not fall. No temptation has seized you except what is common to man, and God is faithful. He will not let you be tempted beyond what you can bear, but when you are tempted, he will also provide a way out so that you can stand up under it" (1 Corinthians 10:12–13).

I felt the strength of the Father and peace by his grace covered me. And into the next church I went. This time I was ready and surely steadfast. And as I was approaching the church, I noticed its beauty from the outside. At the top of the church read *The Church of Sardis,* so as I went through its doors, the church members grabbed me by the hand and said, "Welcome! Come on in and have a seat and enjoy the service with us." So I followed the members in.

We seated ourselves, and as soon as we sat down, all the lights popped off and everybody went to sleep. We were all in the dark. All the members of the church were sleeping—even the man at the altar—all asleep right before my eyes as though dead. This scenario frightened me, so I jumped up and cried, "Okay, no, Lord! Not death again!"

And as I cried out to the Lord, all the members woke up. I got out of my seat to run out of the church, and all the choir members shouted, "Wait! Don't leave us. Where are you going?" they asked.

I just looked back at them, not believing what had just happened. "Please don't leave us," they cried. "We don't get new members often."

"I bet you don't," I spoke. "If you did, how could you possibly notice them here?"

And then one of the members spoke. She said, "Sister, what do you mean? We would really like for you to stay with us. Join us."

They all asked, "Would you?"

I looked at them and I asked, "Why we're you all sleeping?"

And then the man sitting at the altar stood up, and he said, "What do you mean we are sleeping? What are you saying? We do not understand. We do not sleep."

But after he said this, all the members of the church sat down along with the man at the altar and fell asleep again. I thought to myself, *My Lord, how sad is this? How do you begin to keep waking a church up that doesn't even know they are asleep over and over again?*

"Lord," I cried. "Will you look upon this?

And I heard a voice say, "No one knows about that day or hour—not even the angels in heaven nor the Son, but only the Father. Be on guard! Be alert! You do not know when the time will come. Do not sleep. It is like a man going away—he leaves his house and he puts his servant in charge, each with his assigned task, and tells the one at the door to keep watch."

"Therefore, keep watch, because you do not know when the owner of the house will come back, whether in the evening or at midnight, or when the rooster crows, or at dawn. If he comes suddenly, do not let him find you sleeping. What I say to you, I say to everyone. Keep watch!" (Mark 13: 32:37)

So I decided to wake them again, and as I was going around the room waking them, I looked, and I noticed some of the members were even sleeping on their knees at the altar. How sad was this? Sleeping on their knees while praying to the Father. They did not even have the strength to stay awake during prayer. How do you get prayers answered like that? That was a scary thought.

I thought, *Oh my people, will you be asleep when the Father comes back?* This thought had me angry with them, and I went around the room kicking the back of their chairs to wake them up, and again they all woke up, and the choir began singing, and the man at the altar yawned and stood up to speak.

Wow! I thought. *How did he learn his sermon to teach?* As sleepy as he is, this is the saddest church I had ever been in. The man at the altar could not see the sleepy spiritual deadness in his members, because like them, he too was spiritually dead. So I decided to leave, but first I wanted to go to the corner of the church and pray for these members as a whole body. I began to get down on my knees at the altar, close my eyes, and I cried out, "Lord! How long have they been dead and sleeping?"

And I heard a voice speak: "They have been sleeping for a while, so long that they cannot see they are dead inside." The voice continued, "They are only wakened by the open doors for them, and when the doors are closed they will begin to sleep again."

"Oh no! Lord," I cried. "How do I walk out of a life-less church like this, leaving them all asleep?" I felt so empty for them that I began weeping because I knew the Lord is hope, and that their spiritual deadness was because the members failed to keep watch in their house. And over their souls they were missing one or all of the seven spirits of the Lord—the branch from Jesse, the Spirit of the Lord, fear of the Lord, wisdom, knowledge, counsel, and of power which will give them an understanding (Isaiah 11:1–3). Missing any can cause them to not bear fruit.

These are the seven characteristics of the Holy Spirit that rest upon our Christ. The members were praying and singing, yet the church was a morgue full with dead participants, not reaching out for the seven spirits of Christ, putting themselves in danger of Satan taking captive of them, outward looking alive but inward spiritually dead of a deadness of faith and heart.

So I shouted, "Church, you need a rebirth. Repent! And be washed clean with water and the Word. He saves us not because of righteous things we have done, but because of his mercy he saved us through the washing of rebirth and renewal by the Holy Spirit" (Titus 3:5).

"Love the Lord enough to have growth in your heart for him. Wake up, please! So that you can keep watch over your house. The Lord's help is what you need," I cried.

I looked, and they never heard me. *Oh my! You all are in need of uprooting.*

"Repentance and deliverance are what we need. Please, Church, strengthen what is left of God's children," I cried. I then realized I was speaking all alone. *Strength* is what we should cry out for.

"Come on, Church," I cried. "Wake up. Let's ask for strength. We only have one soul, one spirit, and one body. We must protect and keep what we have received and heard from the Father. He is our teacher. He will teach us to keep watch. We should do this by covet endurance and survival with watchfulness."

I began giving thanks to the Father in my prayer for the church because I knew that all the members had to do was repent and strengthen their dead remains.

I began to get up from the altar, and again the members were all asleep. There was no one at the altar to give me a hand. I began shouting out loud again to them, "Wake up, Church!" This time no one heard me. "Wake up, church!" I cried. They all stayed asleep. This time they never woke up, but I began speaking to them anyway, shouting out loud, "You are beautiful on the outside, but inside you are filled with dead men's bones. You are dying! Please wake up!" (Matthew 23:27).

No one heard me. I began weeping again because I knew I would have to be leaving them. I could not stay in a dead church, yet I did not want to leave them like that. This time I started to walk slowly out of the church and sang to them, not wanting to leave them asleep. I was crying out loud, and I heard a voice say, "I know your deeds. You have a reputation of being alive, but you are dead, for it is light that makes everything visible. This is why it is said, 'Wake up, oh sleeper! Rise from the dead, and Christ will shine on you'" (Ephesians 5:14).

IT'S NEVER TOO LATE

"Wake up! Strength is what remains but is about to die, for I have not found your deeds complete in the sight of my God. Remember, therefore, what you have received and heard. Obey it and repent, but if you do not wake up, I will come like a thief, and you will not know at what time I will come to you" (Revelation 3:1–3).

"Amen!" I spoke after I heard this from the voice. I began to leave them, and as I was leaving them, I wanted to look back badly for one last time, hoping they were awake, but I was afraid that they would be still asleep. So I prayed and decided not to look back, and out the doors of the church I went, and as I was heading to the next church, the Church of Philadelphia, I saw what looked like the image of a man driving up in front of the church in that old car in which I had been.

"Wow! I yelled. "What is this?" I walked up to the car, and the man began smiling at me; and when he opened his mouth, a bright light in the car blinded me. I could not see a thing. So I sat down where I was because of the blindness. Wanting to get my sight back, I began praying, and I asked, "Lord why did you blind me?" And I could feel his presence in front of me.

He had gotten out of that old car. The colors from his glory were so beautiful and bright it was almost as if I could see him even with my blind eyes. As I wept, I felt him standing in front of me. He touched me, and then he placed something around my neck.

I tried to touch him back. I just wanted so badly to feel him—feel his touch. I had no fear—none at all. I thought to myself, *I am willing to die for this touch. This touch I had been longing for.* And while I still wept and gasped for breath, because of the excitement I began to feel his hands over my eyes. And immediately I opened my eyes, and the image of the man and the car was gone.

Wow! Where did he go? I thought. I got up and ran into the next church, the Church of Philadelphia. Into the church I went.

"Welcome, sister!" Some of the women met me at the door greeting me. "Welcome to our church," they said with the biggest smiles on their faces.

"Thank you," I replied.

Then one of the ladies looked at me. She spoke, "Oh, I see. I see the Lord is with you."

"What do you mean?" I asked.

She spoke, "Look around your neck. You are wearing the key of David."

"The key of David?" I asked.

The woman said, "Yes! The key of King David is around your neck. This key symbolizes Jesus's authority by which he has opened the doors of the kingdom to all."

The woman added, "You are blessed to wear this key because it has meaning. The one who is holy and true gave you this key."

She kept speaking to me. She said, "Listen to me."

I grew afraid because again I remembered those words from Jezzie's mouth.

But the Spirit spoke and said, "I will place on his shoulder the key to the house of David. What he opens no one can shut, and what he shuts no one can open (Isaiah 22:22). The woman speaks from lightness.

I listened closely, and she said, "Don't be afraid and stop fearing. Your life is between you and your Father."

"The open door is the opportunity for bringing the message of Christ's victory to others. Many will oppose you and your work, but keep speaking the mystery of Christ, and don't worry about those who oppose you, who claim to be like us but are a synagogue of Satan and liars. The Father will make them to come and bow down at your feet and acknowledge that he has loved you" (Revelation 3:9).

The woman then said, "Remember this—what the Lord opens no one can shut, and what he shuts no one can open. I know your deeds. See, I have placed before you an open door that no one can shut. I know that you have little strength, yet you have kept my words and not denied my name" (Revelation 3:7–8).

I looked at the woman and asked, "How you know me like that?" I asked the woman this question because by this time I had learned to test the spirit determined no one else would be putting me in a grave ever again.

So the woman quoted the verse, "It is not I but the Father, the Son, the Holy Spirit who know you. I am just a man speaking what I hear."

So she looked at me and she asked, "Are you ready?"

"Ready for what"? I asked. The woman pulled me into the church, and straight to the altar I went. I was stunned and overjoyed when I looked around, and every member of that church was singing and dancing for the Lord. My Lord, the Holy Spirit was everywhere. People were rejoicing and jumping for joy, celebrating the name of the Lord. I thought I had died and had gone to heaven. I had to keep touching people and myself to make sure this was real.

This church was faithful and loving to the Gospel. I had to check to make sure I had not died and gone to heaven. I was so excited. "Finally, Lord," I cried. "Finally a church that is filled with all the gifts of the spirit. Every member had come together in unity in the body of Christ, as workmen—they were apostles, prophets, evangelists, and teachers. All of God's people at works of service building up into one." The light of Christ filled their smiles.

Oh Lord! I get it. Finally a church with the law of Christ in it. I looked around, and the joy of Christ was on every member's face. His light was glowing and shining like the sun. Bright—their spirit was so bright I was feeling blessed by being there. I grabbed the woman by the hand.

"Oh God!" I shouted. "I like this! I like this!" I joined in and I looked, and even the man at the altar was weeping with his hands in the air calling on the blood of the lamb. Even the children were out of their seats singing and dancing and filled with joy, praising the Lord, looking just like their parents.

The harp began to play, joining in with the piano and the drums. It sounded like I could hear the heavens roar at the sound of the music coming from that church. I looked up, and to top it all off coming down the aisle of the church was the man at the altar. Down the aisle he came, blowing a trumpet, singing "Amazing Grace."

I almost passed out. That was the most wonderful sound I had ever heard. I was so happy that I was floored. I fell to my face completely at the altar in the presence of the Lord. This church had the most beautiful altar I had ever seen with two huge pillars.

One on one side of the altar, and another on the other side of the altar, and in the middle of the altar were two cherubs, one on each side of me. They were solid gold and huge, at least two hundred feet high in the air. When I saw the cherubs, I decided to run in between them. Amazed at their beauty, I ran through the crowd.

Lord, I have to get in the middle of these blessings! Right between the cherubs I was thinking, *maybe fire from the anointing of the cherubs would bless me.* I shouted, "Someone, please let me through!" The members were all over the place, not one in his or her seat.

Wow! I thought. *Let me through, people. Please, people, let me through.* Yet no one would move. It seemed all were enjoying their own presence with the Lord. Enjoying the presence of the Holy Spirit, so I cried, "Oh no, Lord! I want some of this, Lord!" I cried. "Fill me just like them. I need this too, Lord! I am out of my mind for the love of Christ. Let me through, Lord!" I cried.

"Will you look? These people have great love for you and faithfulness like I've never seen. They are all out of their minds."

Then I heard a voice speak. It said, "If we are out of our minds, it is for the sake of God. If we are in our right minds it is for you" (2 Corinthians 5:13).

"Okay, Lord!" I spoke. "I will show you how crazy my love is for you. You've seen *nothing* like this before. Watch this!" I prepared my feet for speed, I stretched my legs for strength, and then I pulled my hair back, determined nothing would stop what I was about to do. "I'll show you, Lord, who is out of her mind. I am getting through. Watch this! Somebody is going to let me through."

I decided to take off running fast, heading in between the two cherubs. Quickly I ran right in their midst. I landed so hard I almost knocked myself out. But I did not care. I just shouted with joy because I made it. I have never felt the presence of the Lord in a church like that in my life. I did not want to leave that church. The Church of Philadelphia is where I would be staying—the church of faithfulness, the church that holds on.

I cried, "Lord, this is where I want to live, never to leave this place. Lord, don't make me leave this church," I cried.

Then he spoke, "I am coming soon. Hold on to what you have so that no one will take your crown. Him who overcomes I will make a pillar in the temple of my God. Never again will he leave it. I will write on him the name of my God , and the name of the city of my God the new Jerusalem, which is coming down out of heaven from my God, and I will also write on him my new name" (Revelation 3:11–12).

I listened, and I could hear the Father calling out my name, "Beautiful!" He called it out three times. I could hear it loudly and clearly. I could not stop crying, when all of a sudden the church doors flew open, again.

"No! No! No!" I cried. "Lord," I asked. "Don't make me leave here."

Then I heard a voice saying, "Do not worry, keep faith," and a huge rainbow began entering through the doors of the church. Coming to get me, it lifted me up, and out the doors it went with me, placing me into the next church, the Church of Laodicea. I guess the Father himself knew he would have to come and take me out of that church because I was not willing to leave on my own.

And the Father came to me. Lifting me up, he placed me in a rainbow of a covenant of peace. The rainbow wrapped around me like a bond of trust and gave me peace. I had no choice but to go, and it was not easy.

I was kicking, screaming, and praying, "No, Lord, no! Please leave me here!" But he did not listen. The Lord took me out anyway against my will and placed me down into another church. This time I found myself seated down in the choir stand, which was different from the other churches. I was puzzled. *Why did the Father place me down into the church choir? What did he want me to see? He placed me in the choir, and right next to the man at the altar. Why was I placed next to him?* I did not understand. So I looked at the man at the altar, and he looked right at me.

Oh my! Was he strange looking! I thought. *Wow! What's going on in this church? Why does this man look so strange?* He looked different from all of the other men at the altars. He was very short with a long face, and with bold, cold black eyes he stared at me, and I stared right back at him. He watched as the rainbow seated me right next to him.

He had the look of not zealously standing for anything. He never smiled. His face was dry with the look of neither being happy nor sad. He looked as though he had lost his passion for the church. With a look of lukewarmness (neither hot nor cold), the whole church had coldness about itself. The man at the altar and all the members of the church looked cold, as if they neither knew how to hate nor love. They all looked creepy to me as they sat and stared and watched me. Everybody was watching me all around the church.

I looked at the man at the altar again, and I felt he did not want to be there—nor did I. I wondered why no one saw me placed into the church carried by the rainbow but the man at the altar.

I asked the Father, "Lord! Why did only the man at the altar see you place me down into the church?"

And I heard a voice speak: "That is because the man at the altar knows the truth, that the rainbow was God's saving mercy—a covenant of peace." The voice told me that whenever the rainbow appears, I will see it and remember the everlasting covenant between God and all living creatures of every kind on earth (Genesis 9:16).

"Lord," I cried out. "Is there a flood coming?"

And he said, "Though the mountains be shaken and the hills be removed, yet my unfailing love for you will not be shaken nor my covenant of peace be removed" (Isaiah 54:10).

I sat quietly, not saying a word, wondering what the Lord was getting ready to do and thinking of a way out, because it sounded like he was about to shake up some things in that church, and I did not want to be a part of the shaking. I cried out to the Father, "Lord! I am only a visitor. I don't even know these people."

And I heard a voice speak: "Daughter! You will be the watchman."

"Oh no! Lord," I said. "I care to neither see nor watch what is about to happen. Please, Lord! Let me out."

Right after I said this, I was bound to my seat. I noticed that I could not move. I thought in my mind, *Oh no! I have been taken captive, and I did not want to be carrying the sins of that church on my back. I had no need for a backpack.*

"Lord," I cried out. "Why are you taking me captive for these people?"

I began looking around the choir stand, and I noticed briers and thorns all around me. I cried out, "Oh Lord, I get it. They are about to be broken because the whole house heart has become obstinate (hardened)."

I spoke, "Lord, whatever is your will, have your way," and I cried out for them, and a backpack was placed on my back, and the choir began playing music—beautiful music—and they all stood up.

I continued to sit, because really and truly I was saddened for them. I did not want to be a part of whatever the Father was about to put them through. Not knowing what to expect out of the decision that the Lord had made, I sat quietly. I could hear everything going on in the church right from the choir stand. My eyes could even see those members who really was soaked and sour—just dry and in a spiritual mess. I could see they were lacking spiritual wisdom and surely understanding. Forgetting the cross!

I was confused and I asked, "Why would my Lord remove me from faithfulness to a dry church like this, placing a backpack on me for them?" I had no understanding about what he was doing. I was in a place where I was so overjoyed with his presence. *What more could the Lord have wanted out of me? Why would the Lord take me from being overjoyed to a place that was spiritually dry?* I wept.

So while the choir was standing and I was weeping, one woman on my left began poking me in the side with her fingernails. "Aweh!" I screamed. "Why did you poke me?"

"Get up!" she said.

"Woman, please leave me alone. Leave me alone!" I was not getting up.

And then the woman asked me, "Woman! What's that on your back? What have you brought into our church?"

Out of fear, I looked at her. I answered, "I don't know what's in the backpack. Maybe you all will know."

I began to get up to get out of that church before anyone else noticed the backpack. I walked in front of the church toward the front of the choir, thinking, *How I am going to get out of this mess?*

I stood in front looking around the church, thinking how fast I could run out and leave this church. I started measuring the front entrance doors in my mind and the time it would take me to get out, but as I was looking, I could not help but notice the beauty of the church.

My Lord! Was it beautiful! It looked like a five-star hotel. The altar was pearl and acacia wood. Every seat in the church was built from stones from the mountains. The windows of the church were designed as a beautiful mosaic and draped down with fine black wool curtains with beautiful strands of silk covering the walls.

Oh my! I thought. *What do I do now? Everybody is watching me.*

Then I heard a voice speak. It said, "You do nothing. Just stand with the backpack on your back, and then you go back and sit down. Don't say a word."

I followed the instruction of the Spirit and walked back to the choir stand. All the members of the church watched me as I walked.

"Lord! I am not going to be able to run out. What do I do now?" I begged. They were all sitting and watching me as though I had something to tell them. They were watching and waiting on me.

I began to pray, and I heard a voice saying, "Just open your mouth."

"What?" I asked the Lord.

"Open your mouth."

I closed my eyes and I opened my mouth, and a voice spoke through me, and what came out of it shocked me. The voice spoke through me, and a song I will never forget rose up out of me. It was called "Great and Marvelous are Your Deeds, Lord."

The Spirit began to sing, and the rest of the choir began singing along with the Spirit. Then all of a sudden, the front doors of the church flew open, and in came a man walking down the aisle coming straight toward the man at the altar.

Immediately the music stopped. The men standing around the man at the altar ran and grabbed the man who entered the church, throwing him to the ground.

"Oh no!" I said. "Don't hurt him. He is a visitor and in need of help." The man who stumbled in looked so sad and in desperate need. His clothes were torn. His hair was knotted up as though it had not been kept in years. I looked and took notice of his feet. He had a shoe missing. He had one shoe on the left foot and nothing on his right foot. He looked cold, tired, hungry, and maybe saddened by a past situation.

I watched the man and could not help but notice his eyes. They were flaming. They had a shine about them, bright like light. He reminded me of the Father.

I screamed for the man: "Hey! Come up here with me. The Lord will come and get us out of this mess!" But the man never spoke a word. He looked at me so sadly it made me sad too. He looked as if he was in need of love, and the church would be where he would want to find it, but I noticed the man was stumbling a little, as though he was not sure about the church and that it might not meet his great needs.

He stumbled as though his heart was hurting, and he knew what was inside the hearts of man. I watched as he got up to walk again. He walked as though he had been walking for days.

"Hey!" I yelled. "Church! Let's give him a drink of water."

No one said a word.

"Wow, people! You really don't want to help the poor man?" No one answered. By that time, the security men for the man at the altar began to throw the stumbling man to the ground again, as if they did not want him to get up.

They asked him, "Who let you into the church grounds?" The man did not answer.

"Oh God!" I prayed. "Have mercy on this man. They are going to hurt him even more than he's already been hurt."

"Lord!" I cried. "Don't let them beat him up!"

Everybody got quiet, and then the man at the altar spoke. He asked the man, "What do you want?"

Finally the man who stumbled in answered: "I am hungry, will you feed me?"

And the man at the altar said, "Do you pay tithes here?" And the man who stumbled in did not say another word.

The man at the altar then asked, "And do you want me to feed you? Are you a member here?"

And the man who stumbled in looked back at the man at the altar with the most beautiful eyes I had ever seen. The fire had sizzled down, and he answered the man at the altar, saying, "Yes I am. I am the body, but yet! When I was sick, you did not pray for me. When I was in prison, you did not come to visit me, and now that I am hungry, you will not feed me? But now that you are rich and have acquired wealth, and you do not need anything, you do not realize that you are wretched, pitiful, poor, blind, and naked" (Revelation 3:17).

THE WITNESS
FOR THE CHURCH

The man began to weep, and then he raised his hand toward heaven as a witness to what was about to happen. As the judge of the church, he spoke, "I AM."

"The *amen* is speaking with authority, and because of your deeds, I am about to spit you out of my mouth." The room of the church filled with quietness, and a splash of fire came from the hands of the man.

He spoke, "Because I am her judge, those whom I love I rebuke and discipline. So be earnest, and repent of your sin" (Revelation 3:19).

"What you carry around is the sin of apathy, living primarily for earthly wealth and selfish desires, showing neither anger nor enthusiasm for your Father (self-centered), making your faith and love toward your Father of secondary importance, and your riches."

First, he began to tell them the parable of the rich fool. He said, "Watch out! Be on your guard against all kinds of greed, because a man's life does not consist in the abundance of his possessions" (Luke 12:15).

"This is how it will be with anyone who stores up things for himself but is not rich toward God." The man warned, "Watch out!" And I fell to my knees after listening to the man, and while on my knees I wept strongly for the church, because I knew he was the judge of the church and speaking harshly to the members of the lukewarm church. I watched with my eyes closely, afraid to take my eyes off him.

As I watched, a raven flew into the church, holding in his beak bread and wine, placing it into the hands of the man at the altar, and he said, "I am the bread of life. He who comes to me will never go hungry, and he who believes in me will never be thirsty" (John 6:35).

I prayed so hard: "Oh Lord, have mercy on us." I said *us* because I was still carrying a heavy backpack on my shoulders that had been placed by the Father.

After I cried out for us, I heard a voice speak: "Yes, cast your bread upon the waters, for after many days you will find it again. Give portions to seven Yes to eight (Jesus). You do not know when disaster may come upon the land. If clouds are full of water, they pour rain upon the earth (miracles will happen), whether a tree falls to the south or to the north, in the place where it falls, there will it lie. Whoever watches the wind? He will not plant. Whoever looks at the clouds will not reap (not crying out to the Lord), as you do not know the path of the wind, or how the body is formed in a mother's womb. So you cannot possibly understand the work of God, the maker of all things."

"Listen closely," he said. "Sow your seed in the morning (fasting) and at evening let not your hands be idle (praying), for you do not know which will succeed whether this or that or whether both will do equally well" (Ecclesiastes 11:1–6). When the man opened his mouth to speak to the man at the altar these things, out of fear all those in the church got out of their seats and asked, "Are you Elijah?"

They began to ask the man, "Where did he come from?" He kept quiet and did not answer them anymore.

So the man at the altar saw the commotion of the church, and he spoke, "Quiet, everyone! Please, this is a trick. Let us not believe what we see."

"Oh my Lord"! I cried. "Did he just say a trick?" Immediately when the man had said this, I fell to my knees again and began to pray for the whole church, because I knew the power of God in my life, and that man who stumbled into this church had the power of God in his eyes. I knew something was about to happen, and soon, on my knees, I stayed flat on my face. I figured if Christ himself had come down into that church to speak, it was not going to be good, and I was right—this was big.

Somebody was going down, and I did not want to go down with them. This time they were on their own. I cried out loudly for help, and then immediately I began to get up, to run out of the church, and I could feel the presence of the Father strongly. I heard what sounded like an earthquake. It began to shake the whole church, rocking back- and forward—the whole church was in rumble. What on earth is this?

In fear I cried, "Oh no, Lord, get me out of here," and I watched, and I noticed the man who stumbled in and kneeled down to write an inscription. He wrote it in bold print. And It read *mene, mene, tekel, parsin* (Daniel 5:25).

I screamed loudly, "Help! Help! I am not going down with them." I remembered that the inscription on the wall that Daniel translated for King Belshazzar meant disobedience and dishonesty was making them neither cold nor hot.

I cried out, "Repent, church, and be saved!" And then all of a sudden the church began shaking, the walls were cracking, and the wind was blowing all over the church. The wind was so strong that all of the glass of the church was blown out. All of the people were trying to hold on to their seats for dear life, but they were not strong enough for the Lord's powerful hands.

So the members were falling and weeping all over the church, shouting for the power of the Father to let go, and I heard a voice speaking loudly: "Disaster! An unheard of disaster is coming. The end has come! The end has come! It has roused itself against you. It has come! Doom has come upon you who dwell in the land. The time has come. The day is near; there is panic, not joy, upon the mountains. I am about to pour out my wrath on you and spend my anger against you. I will judge you according to your conduct and repay you for all your detestable practices among you. Then you will know that it is I, the Lord, who strikes the blow. The day is here! Doom has burst forth, the rod has budded, arrogance has blossomed! (Ezekiel 7:5–10).

Weeping with fear, the members were begging the man to stop with his discipline. I watched closely. I looked up, and he spoke to me, "Daughter! When I placed you as a watchman, you are to speak boldly and warn the house of all its wickedness. You are to speak to the wicked with courage and boldness."

You are to say, "Listen, Church, surely you will die if you don't turn from your wicked ways. Warn him, or speak out to dissuade him from the evil ways in order to save his life. If not, I will hold you accountable for his blood"(Ezekiel 3:18–19).

"Daughter!" the man said. "But if you warn him of his wickedness and he did not turn from his evil ways, he will die for his sin, but you will have saved yourself." And immediately a whirlwind came through and picked the man up, and out of the church he went.

I cried, "Take me with you! Please, sir. Take me with you!" I cried for the man, but he did not listen, and into the whirlwind he went, never speaking another word. It was done. Shakings and whippings were all over the church. The members were all over the place, crying for mercy. I looked up, and all of them had been stripped naked of their clothing. None of them had clothes on, nor could they see they were all blind and naked, with scabs on their eyes.

They were all over the place, touching and feeling the walls of the church, trying to see their way out of the church. "Help! Help!" they all cried. I felt saddened for them.

I wept, and I heard a voice say, "Now listen, you rich people weep and wail, because of the misery that is coming upon you. Your wealth has rotted, and moths have eaten your clothes, and your gold and silver is corrupted. Their corrosion will testify against you and eat your flesh like fire. You have hoarded wealth in the last days" (James 5:1–3).

After the voice spoke these words, I looked on the floor beside me, and there was the man at the altar crawling on his hands and knees. He was crying out loudly, "Lord! You can have all my wealth. Every penny of it belongs to you. Just please give me my eyes back, Lord!" He begged loudly, "Just clothe me, and I will feed your sheep."

"Lord!" the man at the altar cried. "Forgive me of my sins, and I will visit the sick and those in prison."

"Lord!" the man cried. "Cover my members and bless them, and I will teach them better. I will be a testimony for all of them to see that the Father loves us, and when he knocks at the door, and we open it and hear his voice, he will come in. And when he comes in, he will eat with us, and we with him" (Revelation 3:19–21).

I wept and wept when I heard the cry of the man at the altar. He was the first I heard to cry out to the Father. It was a sad thing to see a rich man cry out like that, a man who had it all now crawling on his hands and knees begging for sight. He was now pitiful and poor, now needing the richness of the Lord because he could not help himself. His selfish desires were all gone, and he was now totally dependent on the Lord. Totally naked, he lay there helpless, and all of his members who followed him had also been stripped and without clothes, which was a sad thing to see. I could hardly look at them, least of all know to leave them like that, but I had to do so.

I do not know what else to do, I thought to myself. I will never forget the words out of the man at the altar's mouth. I will never forget the coldness of his eyes and that strange look he had about himself.

I guess one would have to have cold eyes to deny someone food and water, knowing one has much. So I started to leave, and I looked back at the man at the altar. I said, "Sir, let me pray for you," and I grabbed the man by the hands and I began to pray with him.

I said, "I know that the man who straggled into your church loves the church, so don't worry, he will come back again to visit with you, knocking and waiting on you to open the door."

"Sir"! I cried. "He will come back. That's a promise, and he will restore your sight. He will come with salve for your closed eyes so that you will be able to see again. Wait for his arrival, and wait patiently!"

LOOKING BACK ON SO MUCH PAIN

I held on to the man's hand tightly, not wanting to let go. I cried out to him, "Have mercy, Lord! May you give this church mercy?" Then the peace of the Father came upon me and I let go of his hand, and out the doors I went.

"Where now, Lord?" I asked. I sat down on the steps of that church, just looking up to the heavens and trying to get an understanding of the works of the Lord, and then tears began flooding my face—they were unstoppable. I didn't know what else to do but to cry over and over again.

I opened my mouth and reached my hands to the heavens and cried out, "Thank you, Father, for salvation. And thank you for all that I have been through." I said, "Lord! I have been chased by creatures through the woods, almost losing my eyes and my ears. I have been dragged through dirt backward at the speed of lightning, screaming for my life. I had to walk away, abandoning my family, not knowing what else to do, running for dear life, running from the unknown."

I've had my enemy chasing me, the one from the beginning, you know, the one from the garden of Eden. He chased me fast, running side by side with me while trying to defile my body with his deadly sting—his sting of death and sin while he was masquerading as light. Although darkness, he camouflaged himself as light, being the craftiest creature of them all (Genesis 3:1).

Then I had the fight of my life in a storm with Leviathan—the beast of the sea, a beast that tried to destroy me; with fear and all his demonic powers he tried to kill me. Suffering and terror were his name, but I overcame the evil with the blood of the lamb. I then found myself wandering around in a desert—the most deserted and abandoned place I have ever been in my life. I was placed there in a wilderness pilgrimage where I could not move, and it was there where an experience arose. A Spirit led me there to be tempted.

I lay there quietly and watched as another beast arose from underneath the earth, rising up and revealing his entire splendor and power, leaving me wondering who he was. Yet I would soon find out that this beast was no friend of mine, this beast without shame. I soon learned that the beast left me fooled and confused. He made a fool out of me and quickly harmed me without my even knowing that he is the enemy.

He fed me, and I ate. I thought that the bread that beast fed me was the bread of life from my heavenly Father. I ate right from his table right out of his hands. I ate, not knowing that he was one of the henchmen of Satan, all of whom are a package deal. The beast and Satan work hand in hand (Revelation 13:1–18). But thank God for mercy upon me!

Oh, how quickly we will bow down to the enemy by eating right from his hands believing what we see (lust of the flesh). I bowed down to him, and by accepting his food, he left me with a thorn in my side, making me weak and trying to keep me from finishing my journey. I thanked God that this beast did not hurt me.

My Lord! I could never have fought a beast of this huge magnitude I watched him rise up and go down. My thoughts were raging. "Why me, Lord? Why, Lord, would you use little old me to see things of such gratitude?"

"Lord!" I cried. "You placed me in seven churches. The Church of Ephesus (no love) beat me up. The Church of Smyrna (poor and persecuted) tried to chain me down with them. The Church of Pergamum (corrupted), so corrupted they had a fighting man at the altar who knocked me out. The Church of Thyatira (Jezzie) had beds of secrets throughout the whole church. The Church of Sardis (dead), so dead no one could stay awake during services. This church stained my heart, but I overcame the deadness with faithfulness."

"Thank you, Father. You made it all up with the Church of Philadelphia (faithful), so faithful the Lord God himself had to remove me from this church. Then last but not least, the Church of Laodicea (lukewarm), a church so rich but yet about to die—they were no longer able to please the Father. Their richness had hardened their hearts, keeping them from seeing the Lord."

"Lord," I cried. "But you did not let me die. Even when I began to feel that all my hope was gone, you would show up and warm my tired, cold body, never to leave my side."

"Thank you, Father," I cried. "Now what will you do with me? You have promised that the Savior would keep me from the hour of trial that is going to come upon the whole world to test those who live on earth day by day" (Revelation 3:10).

After speaking to the Father, he spoke to me, "Daughter, hold on to what you have. No one will take your crown" (Revelation 3:11).

"Daughter!" he said. "You need to strengthen yourself by trusting me, because I will see you through. What I have shown you is the suffering that is confronting all Christians—the church. There is a battlefield, a war between the church and the beast of the sea (Satan) that is taking place right now. The fiery sea from the first beast is a horrifying warfare that all my children on earth are enduring."

"Listen, daughter, it confronts all, but the church—my bride—with faith will be victorious over the beast" (Revelation 15:1–2). And he gave me a song, a song of thanksgiving to God who alone gives us salvation—the song of Moses—and he sang the song for me, and he placed in my hands a harp. I played the harp.

It was so beautiful. I listened, and he sang, "Great and marvelous are our deeds, Lord God Almighty. Just and true are your ways, King of the ages. Who will not fear you, oh Lord, and bring glory to your name? For you alone are holy. All nations will come and worship before you, for your righteous acts have been revealed" (Revelation 15:3–4).

The Father revealed his deeds to his children. I asked the Lord, "Lord! This vision is great but still without an understanding to me. Please, Lord! Give me counsel so I can rest with this."

And the voice of the Lord spoke, "What I have shown you let no one take or lead you astray." I closed my eyes tightly because I was overwhelmed with it all.

The voice spoke again, "When you go back, there will be much division within the church, which is to place obstacles in your way to turn you from the teaching you have learned."

BE SELF-CONTROLLED AND ALERT

The Lord continued, "Stay away from flattery. It is deceitful and very dangerous. Remember the beast, the beast from under the earth. He is (the religious beast), the beast that will take you to the holy city where you will stand on the highest temple. It will be then and there that he will want you to bow down and worship him. He is very crafty. He has a face of a lamb, yet he speaks of the devil."

"He will look like Christ," the Lord warned, "but talks likes the enemy. It will be then that he will have you questioning whether you are a child of God or a child of the devil, daughter!"

"Watch out," the Lord called out, "because this beast changes from all false religions and spirituality in general into the false prophet and the harlot and becomes a false church—the most deadly form of the religious beast. This beast causes the church to be unfaithful."

The voice of the Lord spoke, "Keep your eyes on watch at all times, testing every spirit, trusting nothing that you see. Keep your armor on and never sit down with it on. You need to stand at all times, keeping watch, and remembering the beast from under the earth. The earthly beast is dangerous, a scoffer who masquerades around the saints because he knows of whom they are—all of them—and he knows every one of them by their names. He is an unholy trinity of wisdom. This wisdom enables Christians to discern how the evil forces of the Devil, both of the sea and of the earth, are active everywhere, always, and at war to destroy the church and her witness to Christ."

Such wisdom comes only from the Father, yet it is a wisdom the Father graciously and richly confers on all his children who listen. I grew a little fearful, but then I could feel the spirit of the Lord hovering over me, and he said, "Get ready!" The voice then ended with amen!

I looked up into heaven and I said, "Lord! Don't leave me. I really need you. Come back and stay with me."

"Lord," I cried. "I cannot imagine you not in my presence when I go back." I slowly stood up, not knowing what was going to happen next. I looked up, and coming up to the church was that old car again. *Woe!* I thought. *Maybe the Lord is going to drive me back home.* I started jumping with joy and then I ran to the car and threw myself in.

As I sat quietly waiting for the car to start, music began playing my favorite song—"Yes, Lord." *Wow!* I thought. *No one knows that this song is my heart but the Lord God Almighty.* I started to sing and pray and praise the Lord.

I said, "Lord, it's me again, and again, and my soul is saying *yes!*"

As I was talking to the Lord, I heard wings flapping in the backseat of the car. *Oh no!* I thought. *What in the world is that flapping noise? Lord, what is that sound?*

I looked up at the rearview mirror toward the backseat of the car to see, and I heard the voice of the Lord say boldly, "Do not look at it!"

This time, hearing the voice of the Lord scared me because he called whatever was in the backseat of the car with me by name. I cried, "Oh no, Lord! I just want to go home! Take me home! How long will I fight this?"

And the voice said, "Daughter, whatever you do, do not let it see fear in your eyes. You will need to take courage and lean on me. Remember all that you have learned from your Savior. It is just a test. You will overcome."

I cut the radio up, and I began to sing louder and louder, trying to block out what was in the backseat of the car. All I could hear was the wings flapping more and more, getting more anxious, as if it could not stand the sound of the Lord's name coming out of my mouth. I thought, *Please, Lord! Tell me that Satan is not in this car with me trying to follow me home.*

Immediately after I had that thought, someone whispered in my ear. He said, "I am! And do not fear." I closed my eyes, not wanting to see what was lying in the backseat of the car. I began singing to the Lord again.

"Lord," I sang. "I will do whatever you want me to do. I will say whatever you want me to say, because my soul says *yes*," and I thanked the Father again for everything. I began calling things as though they were speaking boldly.

I said again, "Lord, I thank you for everything. I thank you, Lord, that I will make it home safe."

"Lord!" I cried. "I thank you for the power given by the seven-fold spirit. With this power I will be able to speak to the Prince of this World that has now given one of his angels the authority to sit in the backseat of my car with destruction on his mind wanting to destroy me!"

I screamed at the creature in the backseat of the car, "You are a liar!" I do not belong to you.

Everything got quiet. The creature laid down his wings in the backseat and sat quietly.

I no longer heard any more movement in the backseat. I spoke, "Lord! Give me the authority to speak to my enemy," and a spirit from heaven came over me.

I said boldly, "In the name of Jesus Christ of Nazareth, Satan, you must flee, and through the blood of the lamb may no weapon be formed against me, or my family shall not prosper."

And the Lord said to me, "You now have the power! Now turn your mirror slowly, and look him eye to eye without fear, and speak!"

Oh my, was my heart beating fast—not because I did not trust God, but I was afraid of what the thing in the backseat of the car looked like. I was wondering if its face would frighten me, so again I began calling out as though it were, because I had faith that the Father had given me, and my faith comes from hearing the message, and the message is heard through the word of Christ. (Romans 10:17).

I touched the rearview mirror of the car, and my hands started to shake. I knew I was not ready, but I had the faith of the Lord with me. I started to move the mirror through faith, but then I heard the voice of the Father, and he said, "Do not touch that mirror until all your fear is gone, keeping your eyes on the Creator and not the creature."

"Lord," I asked. "Are you sure you want me to look it eye to eye? If so, Lord, I will need the eyes of my Father—eyes of fire." I grew obedient to the Lord, and I took a big gasp of air.

"Okay, Lord!" I said. "I am ready." And this time my hands did not shake and my tears dried up. I felt the spirit of boldness rising in me, and then I turned the rearview mirror toward the backseat of the car.

As I looked directly at the backseat, immediately the creature rose slowly. I started talking to my flesh, because my flesh said, *Jump out and run, and as fast as you can*. But my spirit said, *Do not run! Do not fear him.*

The voice of the Lord said boldly, "Here you must die! Daughter, you are now at the cross. Imitating your Fathers humility, your attitude should be the same as that of your Father, your Lord, who being in the very nature of God did not consider equality with God something to be grasped. Still, he made himself nothing, taking the very nature of a servant made in a human likeness. In the appearance of a man, he humbled himself and became obedient to death—even death on a cross" (Philippians 2:5–8).

And the voice of the Lord said, "Daughter, become like your Father. Imitate him."

Immediately, I had to die in the sinful nature of my flesh. I said loudly, "I am not afraid of you." As the creature was rising up in the seat, he breathed upon me, blowing smoke in my face as though he was trying to make me pass out.

I said, "Satan! My Father told me you would be coming because I am faithful. You see, God always goes ahead of me because he is at my right hand. I will not be shaken. Therefore, my heart is glad and my tongue rejoices. My body also will live in hope because my God will not abandon me to the grave, nor will he let the holy ones see decay. He has made known to me the path of life, and he will fill me with joy in your presence" (Acts 2:25–28).

Immediately after I spoke this, the ground started to shake as though an earthquake was coming. I sat quietly waiting on the Lord to conquer for me, and I heard riding horses coming directly toward the car. Loud horses! I looked through the back window because I was thinking, *Lord, what is happening now? Where are the horses going?* I looked out of my window because they were coming faster and faster toward me—a white one, red one, black one, and the last horse was pale, trailing behind the other horses.

"Oh no"! I cried. "What is this?" I was no longer worried about the creature in the backseat because my eyes were now on these giant horses that seemed as big as mountains, larger than all of the seven churches. Standing, I could not believe my eyes and what I was seeing. I screamed and was terrified to the point that I could just pass out, because I did not know what they were and why they were coming for me.

I began to prepare for battle, and something touched me and said, "The battle is not yours—it is mine!" Although I had rest and peace in my heart, I would not take my eyes off the horses. I began to notice they had riders that I could not see. I also noticed the man on the white horse was holding onto something that looked like a rainbow, just like the rainbow that appeared and got me out of the Church of Philadelphia.

He had it in his hand a bow—a weapon of war—and he was coming for me. Nothing was powerful enough to stop him, so I sat and watched, and immediately the white horseman grabbed me and threw me across the back of the horse.

He held on tightly to me, and I just quietly lay on his back, for I knew that horses act as tribulation of the will of the Father. I thanked the Lord for his amazing grace and the peace he leaves with us because peace above man's understanding came over me. I knew the horseman was sent to me to conquer and to bring me victory over my life and over my enemies. I saw in his hand his bow, and in his right hand he carried its representation of earthly warfare, destruction of the enemy, a bond of trust for all of God's children (Revelation 6:1–2).

So by seeing the bow, I could not help but to feel restful. My eyes were closing and I was still, letting God be God. I fell into a deep sleep in which I no longer had control over my body but was in the hand of my Savior. He had given me rest and sleep, and as I slept, the Father showed me amazing things. I recall riding on the white horse going through and through the earth, and as we went through and through the earth, I noticed that the riders of the horses were pouring out something all over the earth. Yet I could not see what they were pouring. When I looked down, though, I could see all the saints throughout the world fighting wars.

Spiritually I could see them fighting, but I could not see *what* they were fighting. Soon I saw that as the saints cried and prayed to the Lord, the white horse rider poured peace and hope out of his right hand and went to battle for them. The saints were unable to see what they were battling, yet the Father saw everything, for he was their conqueror.

THIS BATTLE
IS NOT YOURS

I cried out loud, "Wow, Lord, the saints are fighting, and they don't even know it. Nor can they see you are fighting with them."

I noticed every hand that was raised toward the heavens and every knee that was bowed on earth. The Father poured out peace and hope over them. The white horseman sat pouring and pouring over and over again peace and hope.

I quietly watched, and I could hear prayers—the cries of the saints crying out to the Lord. They made me cry, and I began weeping and weeping. Then I heard the voice of the Lord saying, "My Church, when you go to war against your enemies and see horses and chariots and an army greater than yours, do not be afraid of them because the Lord your God who brought you out of Egypt will be with you. The priest has come forward. Do not be terrified" (Deuteronomy 20:1–4).

I sat quietly but wondered what the other horses were doing. I looked back, and there I saw the fiery red horse and his rider being dreadful. He was riding around with destruction on his hands, taking peace. He was let loose on all the earth, and following him were famine and death being poured out constantly. The earth was in chaos. Everyone was in fear. I looked and I noticed that even with what the destructive horses were doing, the conquer on the white horse continued to battle—battling for the church, battling for the saints—at all times taking capture of the horses who bore the name Destroyer.

I asked, "Lord, will your children be hurt by this?"

And a voice answered, "Do not damage the oil and the wine" (Revelation 6:6).

I cried for the church because of all the pain we are enduring together on earth, and as I wept, I looked up, and riding on the back of the white horseman with me was an angel who wiped every tear from my eyes. As he touched my face, he began to make me laugh. He flew around my ears, tickling me, bouncing up and down on my back, making me laugh, and taking my mind off the struggling saints.

He filled my heart with joy by jumping in midair. He changed his looks over and over again, making me laugh. He was the strangest looking creature I had ever seen. He had hair—lots of it—and he had it parted in the middle of his head. It was as if whatever I thought of his appearance, he would change it to whatever color, whatever face I wanted for him to have. He would do whatever I wanted him to do—anything to bring me joy.

I had so much joy being with him that I laughed myself back to sleep, a very deep sleep—a sleep that felt as if it had been months since I was last awakened.

When I did wake up, I found myself lying on a white pillow with the smell of fragrant incense around me—the most beautiful scent I have ever smelled. I also noticed that my hair was down my back.

My face also was different, and my skin was soft like a peach. My face felt ten years younger without a blemished spot on it. I felt around my neck, which was encircled with jewels, and a beautiful scarf wrapped around me with dangling tassels.

The tassels were the colors of the rainbow held in the hands of the Father. When I stood up, I noticed that I was reclothed in the most beautiful gown I have ever seen, like that of a bride. I had a heavenly smell all over me. It was as though glory had filled me.

I danced and danced, and as I danced I noticed a wheel following me back and forth. The more I danced, the faster the wheels went to and fro, covering my every move.

The Holy Spirit filled me and gave me a Holy Ghost dance. The power of the Father was in me, for I had never danced like that in my life. Joy must have been all over my face. Rejoicing overflowed in my heart.

As I danced, the wheels followed me wherever I went. I looked up to the heavens crying with joy, and rain would come down and then the sun would come out and the rain would come down again, and the sun would follow, as if the Lord was washing me over and over again and giving me glory after glory.

I did not want to stop dancing, but the voice of the Lord spoke, "Daughter! I see your eyes are good, which makes your whole body good."

The voice continued, "You are now ready to go back," and immediately I could hear prayers—lots and lots of them—as though they were coming from heaven.

I fell to my knees, and I could hear them praying loudly and clearly. Wherever the prayers were coming from, they overjoyed my spirit. They really represented heaven. A million saints were praying for me and singing with great victory.

They were all singing together on the right tune.

"Thank you, Lord!" I cried.

And the voice said, "When the saints go marching in, you will be in that number!"

I broke down with tears of joy. I could hear that song clear as light: "Oh, when the saints go marching in, I want to be in that number." *What more could one ask for?* I thought.

Yet I had to go back home quickly because I now knew that as a child of the Lord and the woman of my home and of the Gospel, I needed to get back to them because the enemy anger was against me and my seeds (the church).

I now had a complete understanding of the great need to go home and fight for my family.

The Lord had separated us to strengthen me with the Gospel, filling my heart with the truth. I was ready to go back home. I now knew that the enemy would be waiting for me with hatred (enmity) between my seeds and his (Genesis 3:15). Yet even now, knowing this, I knew I was not to be afraid of what I would be facing.

No devil out of hell would stop me from fighting for my family because my God was with me. I decided that I was not allowing my heart to be troubled (John 14:1), and I was now ready to go back and go to war. I knew my household was not ready, for I had left some unfinished business in my home. I had to go back to them, and I wanted them all ready to march for the kingdom of God. One by one we needed to be ready for when the Lord decided to come to us or decided to call us home to victory.

I walked up to the car again, and this time the engine started on its own. I knew then that the Lord was saying, "It is time to go!" Into the car I went, heading home.

COVENANT FROM THE GARDEN

I spoke, "Lord, you brought me here. I will need you to take me back," and I looked up, and everything was gone. All the churches, the street, and the signs—everything was all gone. I was on a whole new road, all alone. Just my Lord and me, heading back with only one way to go.

I figured this time I would just let the Lord take me back, and he did. The car began driving straight, never stopping nor turning to the right or left. Straight back we went. It is amazing how when completely trusting God our ride becomes smoother with the Father in charge of the road—and our journey.

While riding with him and listening to the voice of the Lord speak, I asked, "Lord, how do I get you to answer me when I pray for my family?"

"Lord," I cried, "my family is one of the seven churches suffering from the seven deadly sins in great need of your holy presence."

"Lord, I have come to you with fasting and prayer, with honor and glory, calling on my kinsman Redeemer to save us from the Evil One."

"Lord, I need my prayers answered—the Word says that you hear the cries of the righteous."

And I heard the voice of the Father say, "Go home, daughter! Shout it aloud! Do not hold back. Raise your voice like a trumpet! Declare to my people their rebellion, and to your household their sins. For day after day they seek me out. They seem eager to know my ways as if they were a nation that does what is right and has not forsaken the commands of its God."

"They ask me for just decisions and seem eager for me to come near them. 'Why have we fasted,' they say, 'and you have not seen it. Why have we humbled ourselves, and you have not noticed?'"

"Yes, on the day of your fasting, you do as you please and exploit all your workers. You are fasting yet end in quarreling and strife and in striking each other with wicked fists. You cannot fast as you do today and expect your voice to be heard on high."

"Is this fast the kind of fast I have chosen only a day for a man to humble himself? Is it only for bowing one's head like a reed and for lying on sackcloth and ashes? Is that what you call a fast? A day acceptable to the Lord?"

The Lord then spoke, "Daughter! I will answer you when you fast and pray. Give to me more than a day of humbleness. Give your Father your all, and everything you think the works of my hands desire of you, by placing every one of your family members in my hands with daily fasting, praying, crying, and rejoicing totally dependent upon me."

"When you do this, it is what I have to loosen the chains of injustice and untie the cords of the yoke to set the oppressed free and break every yoke? Is it not to share your food with the hungry? And to provide the poor wanderer with shelter? When you see the naked, do you not clothe him and not turn away from your own flesh and blood? Then your light will break forth like the dawn and your healing will quickly appear. Then your righteousness will go before you and the glory of the Lord will be your rear guard. Then you will call, and the Lord will answer."

"You will cry for help, and he will say, 'Here am I'" (Isaiah 58:1–9).

"This is true fasting," said the voice of the Lord. "Now get ready, daughter! And remember all that I have shown you. You have not been without on your journey. You needed nothing because I was your provider. I fed you from heaven (spiritual food) and clothed you with a new robe that had been washed."

Then the voice continued, "Now ask anything in my Name, and it shall be given to you."

I replied, "Lord, save my family. Please don't let a one be lost!"

Then I heard the voice of the Lord say amen.

I then asked, "Lord, am I close to home? Because I'm ready now."

He spoke then, "Open your eyes," and I looked, and I was back home where I had begun my journey in front of those woods where the enemy had met me before. I was sitting in the same spot. I got out of the car and began to walk, not knowing which way to go this time.

I felt different. My whole body felt strange, and I was hot all over. I thought to myself, *Lord! What is Satan up to now? He's crafty, you know.*

I looked down, and I noticed my head was on backward because I was looking down at the heels of my feet. The whole backside of my feet and my back were facing me. I had to laugh at myself.

My Lord! I thought. *The Word said he will strike my heel, but my Father the Messiah (Christ) will crush his head* (Genesis 3:15).

I questioned the enemy: "What are you up to now?" I knew it was the enemy again trying to put fear in me, for he is the heel striker. I kept walking backward, determined I would get the last laugh out of the tempter's terror. I knew he was only here to terrorize me.

Yet this time I was not going to fear, because by now I was feeling good about what the Word said, and I was going to stand on it. And that is "If God is for me, who can be against me?"

"God is not a man that he can lie." I spoke boldly: "Satan! It is done. I am going home to my family, and I will not fear!" I yelled it out loud, because by this time, after all I had been through with the enemy, I began shouting, "O Lord! I call to you; come quickly to me" (Psalm 141:1).

I was really feeling the hate between him and me. I cried out loud to the Father because I was thinking, *Lord, I cannot go home to my family like this. They will not listen to me shouting out loud and not holding back, raising my voice like a trumpet declaring to them their rebellion.*

"Lord! They will laugh at me, thinking, *How can she tell us about ourselves, when her own head is on backward?*"

"Lord!" I cried. "Make him stop!"

"He never stops. He will be deadly until the end." And the Lord spoke, "His doom is near. Stay strong and courageous. Remember he roams to and from earth, filled with fury looking to defile. Remember you are a testimony, and he knows when you are losing strength."

I thanked God that the accuser (the Devil) can never accuse me again before God, because he was overcome by the blood of the lamb and by the word of the testimony. I was thankful because I now knew that we will all overcome the enemy with our testimony of Christ (Revelation 12:11). I prayed. I said, "Lord, the word says '*Woe* to the earth and the sea, because the devil has gone down to you!'"

"He is filled with fury because he knows that his time is short" (Revelation 12:12).

I knew judgment is his and for his angels. "Abba! Abba!" I cried. "I am going home. With death on me and my head on backward, I am constantly looking behind me."

I spoke quietly to Abba, "What do I do now, Father? I will do whatever you tell me to do."

And the Lord spoke, "What then shall we say in response to this? If God is for us who can be against us? He who did not spare his own Son but gave him up for us all, how will he not also, along with him, graciously give us all things? Who will bring any charges against those whom God has chosen? It is God who justifies? Who is he that condemns?"

"Christ Jesus who died more than that, who was raised to life, is at the right hand of God and is also interceding for us. Who shall separate us from the love of Christ? Shall it be trouble or hardship or persecution or famine or nakedness or danger or the sword? As it is written for your sake, we face death all day long. We are considered as sheep to be slaughtered."

"No, in all these things we are more than conquers through him who loves us, namely Jesus (Romans 8:31–37)." So then, because I no longer had any fear of what the enemy was trying to do, I kept walking and walking and walking until I noticed that night was coming.

I looked, and a man was in the woods chopping down a tree. "Where are you going?" he asked. I said, "I am trying to find my way home while it is still day so that I don't stumble when night falls.

The man said, "A man who walks by day will not stumble, for he sees by the world's light. It is when he walks by night that he stumbles, for he has no light. You are correct," and the man went back to cutting down the tree.

I started to walk again, and a loud shout came from the man's mouth. He asked, "Do you not know why your head is on backward?"

I turned around and walked back to the man. "No, I answered. "I don't quite understand why my head is on backward, but I do know that the Father is able!"

The man smiled. "Yes!" he said. "The Father is able to do all things according to his word. You are walking backward because you are heading home, still holding on to the past. The past will be your stumbling block. You will need to let go! Let go!—of every hurt and pain that caused your journey. Look ahead of you."

"How do I do that when there is so much pain?"

The man said, "You must not become a stumbling block to your family. Remember, accept him whose faith is weak, without passing judgment on disputable matters. Who are you to judge someone else's servant? To his own master he stands or falls, and he will stand. For the Lord is able to make him stand" (Romans 14:1–4).

"If you do not this, you will begin to walk backward again, not being able to see what is ahead of you—nor will you see the blessing that Christ has for you."

"Remember, daughter. Go into your home with caution, carefully ministering to the weak, the unloved, the persecuted, the compromising, the corrupt, the dead, the unfaithful, and the lukewarm, never forgetting this is the Church."

"All of God's children are under danger of the sins of death. The temptation of it will always be there to tone down Christian faith and the truth, which will lead to denying Christ." The cross.

I started to walk again, and he shouted loudly, "Again, Who is this coming up from the desert leaning on her lover? Under the apple tree I roused you there your mother conceived you. There she who was in labor gave birth to you. And then placed me like a seal over your heart. Like a seal on your arm. For love is as strong as death, its jealousy unyielding as the grave. It burns like blazing fire, like a mighty flame. Many waters cannot quench love, rivers cannot wash it away, if one were to give all the wealth of his house for love it would be utterly scorned. (Song of Songs 8:5-7) as the man was still speaking. I began to hear dogs barking loud. I looked and could not see them.

I turned around again, and he spoke, watch out for those dogs those men who do evil, those manipulator of the flesh. (Philippans 3:2) the man began to close his eye's he said. I since the enemy still does not want to let you go. Do not fear! Be strong. The enemy from out of the sea, and underneight the earth is growing in wisdom and power. "I grew quiet because the man was speaking with fire. He said, "Your journey was about you—not your family—any testimony I give to my chosen ones is about them,"Oh my God!" I cried.

The man spoke, "Be strong. This testimony will come with great gifts. Your enemy is growing. He has seven heads—heads represented by his wisdom. He has ten horns that are represented by his power, so do not take him for granted, yet do not fear. he is getting drunk with the blood of the saints, the blood of those who bore testimony to Jesus" (Revelation 17: 6).

"But know that your God is greater in power. My church is crying out to me and I am listening, but when I come to answer what do I see. Lots and lots of adultery. My children are committing adultery with the enemy and his henchman, but yet they cry out to me!"

"Why should your Father answer them when they don't listen to me? Daughter, shout it out loud. Do not hold back. Raise your voice like a trumpet. Declare to my people their rebellion. Tell them they are intoxicated with the wine of her adulteries and their hands are filled with abominable things and the filth of her adulteries."

And then the man concluded, "Amen."

I was so afraid of the hard words the man had spoken.

"Do not be afraid," he said. "Come out of her, my people, so that you will not share in her sins, so that you will not receive any of her plagues. Her sins are piled up to heaven, and God has remembered her crimes. Give back to her as she has given. Pay her back double for what she has done. Mix her a double portion from her own cup. Give her as much torture and grief as the glory and luxury she gave herself" (Revelation 17:4–7).

I was astonished that my God saw me as a prostitute, yet I was guilty of bowing down to the henchmen, thinking more of myself. I thought, *I was going back home to tell my family about their rebellion, but my Father said it was also about me.* I wept and thanked the man and started to walk toward my house, but I noticed my head was still backward. Even so, I knew that everything would be all right because when the Father searched my heart and saw that I was truly ready and sincerely grateful, he would straighten me out on his time and not mine.

So I kept walking, and I walked about a mile into the woods. I looked and noticed that everything was straight. My head was suddenly facing the right direction.

I jumped with joy, shouting out loud to the king of glory: "I love you, oh King, how I love you!"and I heard a voice say! Only a dog return to its vomit, and a pig that is washed goes back to her wallowing in the mud.(2 Peter 2:22) for a man is a slave to whatever has mastered him.(2 Peter 2:19) I answered. Lord I will not go back to the old.

And peace came over me. I looked, and I noticed my home as I had left it, waiting on my presence. I just stood and gazed at it, not moving. I felt that I had been gone so long and found myself in a daze. I was in dying need to see my family again.

As I stood praying for my family, I heard a voice say, "Go home, and there you will know that I have been with them. You will find fruits and lots of them. The fruits are there to remind you of how your life should be."

"Eat," the voice said, "and be thankful in everything. Mercy has been given to you. Grace and truth are your life."

I walked up to the house and saw fruit hanging everywhere, on every tree—just as the Lord had promised. I was overwhelmed, yet I ate all the fruit I wanted. Soon, I noticed my house seemed empty.

THE FRUIT
OF THE SPIRIT

I heard the voice of the Lord saying, "The harvest is plentiful but the workers are few."

I would need to go into my own home like a lamb among wolves with nothing in my hand, no purse or sandals on my feet. I was barefooted but yet clothed. I opened the doors of my home and I spoke, "Peace!"

I shouted louder, "Peace!" It seemed like I could hear lightning over the roof of my house. The power of my God had given me authority to trample on snakes and scorpions and to overcome all the power of the enemy. "Even the demons will submit to you" (Luke 10:1-20).

I knew that now with this authority given to me—I being the woman of my household—nothing would get in my way. I walked through every room, every place in my home shouting out with authority. I called out to every bond that had been holding onto my family for years. I called out every generation's curse that we had to pay for; one by one I called them out with boldness. I was not ashamed, nor am I ashamed now.

All of those spirits were dwelling in my family—almost all of them destroying our lives. I cried, "Spirit of darkness and depression; mental illness and confusion; suicide, murder, lying, HIV, and AIDS; drug addiction, jail, and imprisonment; gambling addiction, sex addiction, sexual immorality, prostitution, adultery, idolatry, homosexuality, lesbianism, and the most dangerous of them all—spirit of Nicolaitans, the spirit from the Church of Pergamum (compromising spirit). The spirit that teaches that you should keep on sinning and all you have to do is repent over and over again, living with no fear of the sword of the Father's mouth (judgment)—no fear of condemnation!"

I went to war, screaming and crying, fighting armed up, just my Father and me. I walked the floors of my home, back and forth, just praying, crying to the rooftop.

"Father"! I cried. "Somebody broke faith with you. Who was it? What generation broke faith, bowing down to other Gods?"

"Have we all not one Father?" I asked. One God created us all. Somebody had broken faith, and my generation was left holding the baggage, paying for unfaithful generations. I decided it did not matter who had stopped praying. The bondage was ending here, right now with me.

I was placing myself before the Lord, and not realizing it was on an altar for sacrifices. I began to faint, and as I was fainting, something grabbed me and lifted me up. I became a little girl again of ten, and I could see myself riding a bike, and a hand was over me at all times—my special friend—and his name was Jesus. I would talk to him day and night. He would talk to me, and I would listen. We would talk about death.

Death was calling my family, and quickly—young and old, male and female. My father's sisters and brother were dying off, leaving us one by one. Leaving us without understanding or knowledge about what the Father was doing, but even at ten I knew something was wrong with this family. Still I did not understand what was wrong. The spirit of death was on my father's generation, and it was determined not to let go.

So when death was hitting and one of my favorite uncles died at the age of fifty, I cried to the only friend I had. I would call him *Yahweh* because even at ten, I knew there was power in that name. I would sit in church and watch as the members of the church cried out to the Father, speaking in tongues and languages that I could not understand. I cried to my friend to have what the members of that church had. I wanted to speak a language that only my friend and I under-stood—that is what the Father gave me.

So, at ten, I walked up to an altar call one Sunday morning, and something came over me. The Lord put a spirit in me that gave me a different language, a language that I could understand. I stood at that altar in what must have been hours with no one to move me.

All of a sudden something touched me, and I passed out. I woke up flying over Jerusalem in a helicopter, crying out loud with tears of joy. As I looked down at Jerusalem, I could see the Father's hands wrapped around the city—the most beautiful sight I had ever witnessed—the same hand that had been wrapped around me was wrapped around this city.

The helicopter soon landed, placing me right in front of a gate. I got out, and what looked like an image of a man met me and wrapped me in a garment and grabbed me by the hand. "Welcome, daughter," he said.

And I cried out, "Are you Yahweh?"

When he said "Welcome, daughter" again, I wept.

He said, "Come see."

When I went with him, I noticed that even at ten I had no fear. I did not care where he was taking me. All I knew was that there was love and light in him for which I had love in my heart.

I was willing to go wherever he wanted me to go. The man took me to a garden—the most beautiful garden I had ever seen. It was filled with butterflies and bees and all kinds of creatures. "Are you hungry?" he asked.

"Yes," I replied.

"Let us eat then." We sat under a huge tree that had all kinds of fruit on it, at least twelve different kinds.

"Pick one," the man said.

I looked at him and I said, "Sir, will you pick one for me because I like them all. You will know what's best for me."

The man said, "Yes, I will decide for you," and he grabbed exactly what I would like and gave it to me to eat—the biggest red, juicy pomegranate I had ever seen.

Excited, I asked, "Sir, will you open it for me?"

He smiled and said, "Yes, not only will I open the fruitfulness in your life, but I will open many doors for you—because you are the apple of my eye and the joy of my ways."

As I was filling my mouth with the juicy fruit, the man kept on speaking to me, saying, "You will call me, and I will answer. You will go astray, and I will find you. You will fall, and I will catch you.

I said, "Sir, am I going to fall when I go back? Because I don't like falling. Sometimes it hurts."

And the man said, "It is okay to fall because the hurts make you stronger. We all have to go down in order to go up. Earth is down and heaven is up. Your heavenly Father went down so you can go up, and as long as you are on earth you will feel like you are falling. Remember to keep your eyes on what is up, which is where your help will come from."

I began to weep again, and the man asked, "Why do you cry?" As if he did not know!

BLESSED FROM THE BEGINNING

And I asked, "Sir, why do I love you such?"

The man held on to me, so tightly that he did not let go. He answered, "This is for me and you. I will bless your life, gifting you with the gifts of the Spirit. You will see that people will find you strange because your eyes will be light, and the world is filled with darkness. You will be just like your Father—with light."

The man continued, "You will be the glue that will hold your family together. They will all know me and seek me one by one. I will call them by name, and they will answer me. I will remove their stone hearts and turn them into hearts of flesh. They shall not worship the stars, the sun, or the moon, for they will know that I AM is their God.

I lay my head on my lap because I was not seeing or understanding all that the man was saying.

He spoke, "Open your hands. I have some gifts for you."

I began to raise my eyes up, but the light was so bright I could not see. Then I noticed a crown on his head—a crown with twelve beautiful stones. Wow! Were they beautiful! They shone brightly. I said, "Wow! I want one of those." I pointed at the crown. "Is this the gift you have for me?"

He smiled and then spoke, "Daughter, these crowns come with death."

"Death," I cried. "You mean I will have to die to get my gifts? Is it that crown?"

After I asked the question, something powerful came over me. The fear of death was no more. With the biggest smile on my face, I said, "Okay, sir. I am willing to die, but please don't let me know how and when I will be dying for death is the destiny of every man.

And he watched as I closed my eyes, and nothing happened. I opened my eyes, and he still was smiling. So I would close my eyes again, and nothing would happen. Finally I opened my eyes and spoke, "Are you going to give me my gift or not? Because you promised, and I am still alive."

Finally, the man opened his mouth to speak, and he said, "You are alive, but for Christ Jesus you will always be in danger of death so that the life of your Father can always be seen in you. The man went on. "Daughter, you will die, but it will be for my name's sake, but I will raise you up and into my presence so you can benefit from eternal glory."

I looked up at the man, and this time I said, "Is it then that I will receive my crown?" He smiled.

I asked, "Can you at least let me see if it will fit my head?" He smiled.

"Sir," I said, "Since you will not allow me to see if it will fit my head, let me at least tell you how I want my crown to be." I told the man that I wanted a huge one—so big I could hardly carry it on my head, and I would need someone to help me hold it up while I walk.

I added, "As a matter of fact, I want my crown to have all the names of my family on it."

The man smiled. He said, "Yes, you will receive what you desire. Then he asked, "Are you ready to go back?"

I said, "Not really, but if I have to, I will."

He spoke, "Let us go. It is not yet the hour for you, but do not worry. Trust me. I will be back to send you on a new journey. This journey will be the one that will be most pleasing to my eyes."

I shouted, "Wow! Do it now! Do it now!"

He smiled and said, "You are not ready for this one. It will be a long and hard one, but you will make it through with long-suffering."

Then he raised his hand to pick another fruit for me. "Here! Eat again!"

I replied, "There are eleven more different kinds of fruit. Will I need all twelve to be full?"

"Yes," he answered. "Not one fruit of your spirit shall be missing. All twelve are needed to keep you full." And he picked and I ate, and he watched me. He never took his eyes off me, making sure I had a taste of all twelve fruits from that tree. The man began to place me back on my way in the helicopter. As I went up, he smiled. I waved at the man, and the man's hand waved back.

I cried out, "Wait! What is your name?"

And he spoke, "I have many; you will learn them."

And I woke up from the altar of the church, not remembering anything about the vision. God had erased every part of it completely from my mind. I got up off the floor of that altar, completely blanked out. It was not until now I understand and remember what happened to me—an experience that arose in my life.

The Father placed me on my journey, the one he had promised me at ten. This journey would be my testimony. It was then and there I would be a witness for Christ. You see, the Savior fed me from only one tree. I had no choice but to eat from the tree of life. He picked, and I ate, and we both were happy. This was a covenant between my Savior and me. At ten I was poor in spirit.

Being poor in spirit (meaning totally dependent on the Lord), he had given me the blessing of the kingdom of heaven. I mourned (and the Father gave me comfort by holding my hand). I was meek, and humble (leaving me without pride), so my inheritance was the earth. Everything I touched was blessed. I was hungry and thirsty for Yahweh. I would look for him, wanting to talk and make him my friend (and he fed me from twelve crops of fruit.)

I was merciful (I considered my family for the kingdom—the church—wanting all their names on my crown). I was pure in heart (I saw the Savior), and he himself promised me a victorious life—the crown of external life. I had peace being in his presence because I had no fear.

I held the man accountable for his promise. I knew he could not lie. I was persecuted and tested to see if I was willing to die for what was righteous at any given minute, and I was willing, yet the Father told me it was not yet my hour.

All of this made my heart right at that time with the Savior to receive the blessing. Thank you, Jesus, for the gift of holiness and truth. The holy spirit is the gift of life given by Christ.

I now knew that this was powerful—the power that God had given me right into my own hands. The hands of a woman and her seeds. I woke up lying on the floor of my closet, in my own home. It was where I would always pray. I now remembered what happened to me. I woke up one day from prayer with the Lord. He called my name that day, and I answered, "Here I am, Lord!"

Then he placed what looked like a large backpack on my back. It weighed me down just a little, but I did not care. I was willing to carry it with the help of the Lord's graceful hands.

The backpack was placed on my back for all the family to see. The baggage that I was carrying was all the rebellion and despicable sins that weighed me down. The Lord had had enough. He packed me up and separated me from my family.

I remember that I was to head in the direction of the Father, and I would be all alone, not knowing what he was doing in my life. I called on God, night and day, crying out, "Here I am, Lord! Here I am!"

I thought the Lord would never answer me. My days turned into nights, and my nights turned into days. I could hardly wait until night came to cover me because I was beginning to believe that it was the only time the Father would listen to me. I would toss and turn all night long, begging and pleading for the Lord to take this thorn from my side, a thorn of weakness and pain, but he would not.

I had a beast on my back. He was in my backpack eating at my flesh. I was struggling with the beast and confused about why the Lord allowed him to eat at my flesh night and day. I loved the Lord with all my heart and soul. Why would he allow me so much pain? But yet! Even with my struggles, I knew that my God had not left me. I knew it was something missing in my life, and that God was trying to tell me something—the spirit that I was missing. I did not know at ten that I was so beautiful and fruitful to the Father. Not missing a fruit, I was thinking now as a woman what had happened to me and what I was missing that made me incomplete with my Father.

SINNERS WILL TURN AGAINST THE HOUSE OF PRAYER

It was then the Lord showed me the vision. He spoke, "Daughter! You were missing gifts—gifts from the Holy Spirit that you need. There are seven in all, and you need all seven to complete this journey. You will need me, the Lord your God Almighty! The fear of the Lord—knowledge, understanding, counseling, and wisdom—which comes with power."

I asked the Lord, "Lord! Then which one am I lacking to become complete and made whole as you require of me?"

And then the power of the Lord covered me. He began to counsel me, saying, "Daughter! If you accept my words, store up my commands in you. Turn your ears to listen to my wisdom and apply understanding. Then call out for insight, and cry loudly for understanding! Look for it as if it were silver, and search for it as if it were a hidden treasure."

"Then you will know to fear the Lord, and there you will find the knowledge and understanding of your

God. There he holds victorious insight for the upright. He will shield those who walk blameless, and he guards the course of the just."

"Protect the way of the faithful ones, and then you will understand what is right, just, fair in every good path, for wisdom will enter your heart and knowledge will please your soul. Discretion will protect you and understanding will guard you" (Proverbs 2:1–11).

I called out for some time and then passed out from crying and calling night and day.

The Word said that I had to search for wisdom like a hidden treasure. I never stopped looking for the promise, holding on to the Lord's promise. He does not lie.

I headed on my journey with an open mind, believing that I am a believer. I decided that I would no longer call myself just a Christian. It was not enough for me because Christians act any kind of way. My journey made me not just a Christian, but also a true believer with the backpack placed on my shoulders, given by the Father who truly showed me that I belong to Christ. I am a child of the Son of the living God (Jesus Christ).

I now had insight into what the Savior was showing me. He needed to show me some things that I had no understanding of, and he did show me! That there were two types of children—one who is his and one who is not. The one who is not has another Father, the Father of the Beast of the Sea, and from underneath the earth. He wanted me to have no parts with him. The Lord knew that in order to complete me with knowledge and understanding of my journey, he had to teach me right from wrong by allowing me to be separate from everyone and everything in my life, and it was so hard. It would be one on one with my Father—just the Lord and I.

When my journey was over, I now understood the difference in Christians and believers. I realized that just being a Christian was not good enough. I was wrong if I was only a Christian and not a believer. It would have made me an orphan—one who did not know where they belong. No destination. The Lord knew I had to find my way, and he used the churches to show me some things. I had been blown and tossed by the wind. A double-minded man, unstable in all my ways, lacking wisdom—the Lord allowed a testing of my faith to show me his glory (James 1:2–8).

Church by church, the Father showed me what was inside of me, giving me insight into what he sees. Throughout the churches, I noticed that the Christians were lacking love and understanding, and believers loved everyone. Christians feared every attack of the devil, and believers trust God even when trials arrive. Christians compromise. They eat from both tables by making many excuses for the wrongs they can easily turn into right, then they hate the discipline that the Father gives them, always blaming the devil.

The believers know it is either wrong or right and there is no in-between. Many Christians ignore the first command of the Lord—to love him with all their heart and soul—and the second command is to love their neighbors. Also, Christians walk away from the love of Christ at any given time, falling out of love so easily when things are not right.

Believers, on the other hand, test all spirits with understanding and knowledge of the truth. Christians' eyes are easily darkened, causing them to become spiritually dead, remembering nothing that the Word has spoken to them, yet believers are alive because Christ lives in them.

Christians are faithful to the church, meeting up every Sunday, faithfully becoming traditional and religious. Believers are faithful to Christ because they believe that they are the church standing firm. Christians are sometimes on fire for Christ, but yet! So easy it is to turn cold while in a storm or trials and maintain wariness at all times. Believers are always on fire in the Word, learning to meditate on it day and night.

Never letting the fire burn out, trusting every word from the book of life, and holding God up to his promise—this was my wisdom that was given to me by Christ as a gift. Now I knew how to get the beast off my back. I now know the truth. The church begins with the seed of the woman (Revelation 17)—the woman on the beast, the enemy that is causing the church so much pain.

The Lord blessed me to take a stand. He said, "Why is the woman carrying on like this? She is the church! And because of her behavior, now the whole world ignores her (the church). She is despised and rejected and persecuted by people in the world under the motivation of the harlot and the beast. The world sees how she behaves, and no one wants to follow her destructive ways.

She denounces the world and its lifestyle of unbelief and ungodliness as she witnesses to the only true God and Savior, the Christ (Revelation 11:3–10).

I asked the Lord, "What now?"

And a voice spoke loudly to me, saying that the sinners will turn against the house of prayer (the church), attempting to destroy it, the holy city, and God (the church). The voice of the Lord spoke, "Listen, Church. The woman (harlot) is supposed to represent for Christ the church (the Gospel), but what is she doing with all her beauty? She is now a prostitute, prostituting herself out and becoming the pseudo-church. While appearing to be beautiful, she accepts the honor of the world. She flatters and encourages the lifestyle of the ungodly. She loves the world, money, and flashy things that will all bring the judgment of God upon her and her children's lives" (Revelation 18:3–9:15).

A TREASURE
IN A JAR OF CLAY

I began to weep so hard that I could no longer see. "Lord! Stand by us. Please, Lord, stand by us. We love you, Lord!" I cried out. "The harlot sits upon many waters" (Revelation 17:1).

The waters are the people and crowds and nations and tongues on which she sits. The woman has caused the whole world to be punished. John says, "Come. I will show you the punishment of the great prostitute who sits on many waters. With her, the kings of the earth commit adultery and the inhabitants of the earth were intoxicated with the wine of her adulteries."

"Oh my God!" I cried. I was finally able to see what the Father was showing me—the church was prostituting itself out, which John foresaw, and he was astonished at what he had seen (Revelation 17:6). The church is riding on the beast. The church is riding the enemy of God saints on earth,. I wept because of the understanding the Father had given me, because I now had understanding of the beast of the sea (the political beast)— the powerful government, economic, and societal beast and the knowledge of the antichrist that has risen in the church. Together, all of these forces were waging war against God's children, the blood of the lamb.

As I thanked the Lord, I heard a voice say, "This, daughter, calls for the mind of wisdom."

The voice then said, "You will now go back home to your family, and one by one you will bless them with the Gospel of truth. It is why I allowed the testing, and yes, you, a woman fighting for the family."

"You will share the Gospel with your seeds (the church)." I fell to my knees day and night, and one day the doors opened for me to go back home. I lifted my hands to the heavens and allowed the presence of the Holy Spirit to reign in me.

And he spoke, "Blessed is the man who perseveres under trial. Because he has stood the test, he will receive the crown of life that God has promised to those who love him" (James 1:12).

This is my testimony. I became the Church of Smyrna. I was led into the desert by a spirit. It was there that the Lord prepared a place for me. I found myself with the dragon standing before me. I was persecuted by the beast of the sea, the government, which caused me to be poor in spirit and totally dependent on God. The devil put me in prison. I found myself fearing what I was about to suffer—not wanting to be tested, not wanting to suffer in the hands of the enemy, my accuser. It was there that the Lord gave me wings like an eagle. He nursed me in the presence of my enemy time after time and a half times, showing my enemy that he could never accuse me again.

"Daughter, stay faithful until death," the Lord whispered in my ears. "This you will overcome." Without a clear understanding, I was blinded and I could not see, so I went kicking and screaming, not wanting to go, until finally the Lord dragged me by the hairs of my head.

"Daughter," he spoke. "You mess yourself up and now I will correct you, and it will be there that I will nurse you in the presence of your enemy."

Through bristles and thorns I went, and it was then that the Lord became my counselor. He said, "Behold! I am the true vine, and my Father is the gardener. He cuts off every branch in me that bore no fruit while every branch that does bear fruit he prunes so that it will be even more fruitful" (John 15:1).

And the pruning began. The Lord cut and cut and cut until I was no more. He had gotten rid of *me*, and there is where he made me new—a new creature with no more condemnation. When he finished me, there was no more sea (sin). The beast was gone, and the smell of death was no more. As my Father did for me, I did also.

I conquered death, Hades, and the grave through the blood of the testimony of Christ. I was forgiven and never forsaken. I persevered through my trials, not one day losing faith. It was there during my trials I learned the many names of the man in the garden. He is the Great I Am, my King, my Lord and Savior, my Refuge when I have committed a crime, my Counselor, Yahweh, my Master, my Rabbi, my High Priest, Hosanna (who saves), my Revelation, and above all names, *my will to live*. He never let go of me—he called out my name as Beautiful! He asked me, "Who do you say I am?"

I now had understanding of who he is. I answered, "You are the Christ, the Son of the living God!"

And he spoke on this mountain: "My children, I built my church, and it will stand—the New Jerusalem. Keep watch! My children, keep watch over your houses!"

I love the Lord so much. He turned my journey into a training camp for me and blessed me with his teachings. I was put in a place with nothing but women (a church) and placed before me was every spirit of the seven churches, blessing me to see what they look like in detail, these seven women.

Seven churches crossed my path along with the two beasts. My God is good. I began to bear fruit—twelve crops of fruit, all the fruit of spirit arose in me.

"Now I can work in you," the Lord spoke. "Now I can work through you. It is time for your eyes to see and for your ears to hear what the Spirit says to the churches. You will enter into the doors that have been opened for you, which is your revelation, where you will receive good gifts from the Father."

In order to be chosen by God, we all must prove our faith, and proving our faith is a blessing and a test. And we will all have to pass the test. One by one, we will all be tested. This is where some of us fail because of what is in us, the good with the evil. God has the need to test his children. We have to be willing to receive and accept the invitation, because all our power comes from God.

We own nothing. We are a treasure to the Lord; and because we have this treasure in jars of clay to show that this all-surpassing power is from God and not from us, we are hard pressed on every side but not crushed, perplexed but not in despair, persecuted but not abandoned, struck down but not destroyed (2 Corinthians 4:7–9), knowing that God is the tester, and testing is for our good.

Satan is the tempter (evil), and by our own evil desires when tempted, we are dragged into sin (James 1:13–18). God gives good and perfect gifts from above to his children, and this testimony was my perfect gift from my Father. We must be encouraged in heart and united in love so that we may have the full riches of complete understanding.

That you may know the mystery of God, namely Christ, in whom are hidden all the treasures of wisdom and knowledge (Colossians 2:2–3). So when the Tempter comes, remember he is a mocker, deceiver, impostor, scorner, hypocrite, a folly that is vanity (empty) and full of falseness and silliness. The female folly is loud. She is undisciplined and without knowledge. She sits at the door of her house on a seat at the highest point of the city calling out to those who pass by who go straight on their way (Proverbs 9:13–15).

Saints, remember the beast. Pay him back and do not worship him. Do not commit adultery with her, and do not buy her cargo anymore. Come out of her. My people pay her back double for what she has done (Revelation 18:1–8). Be watchmen for your houses! The Lord holds us accountable for the sins of our homes by placing backpacks on us for everyone to see our sins. We are the church, the offspring of Christ, and our tests are only to cause us to bear fruit and to be nursed by our Father time after time again. Satan wages war, but yet! The chosen and faithful followers will overcome.

I end my testimony with the following: I petitioned the heavens with prayer and fasting and in sackcloth and ashes. I asked the Father of the heavens, the earth, and the sea, and everything in it with tears in my eyes. I asked, "Does my DNA match yours?" And silence was given to me, and I could hear the angels singing for a short while.

Then all of a sudden, I could feel the wind blowing. The wind began to blow through my hair, as if someone was brushing it, and a voice spoke, "I am one hundred percent sure you are mine. The test results are in, and you are a child of the living God!"

Immediately, I fell to my knees and thanked him. You see, when I arrived back home, the Nephilims were already gone—they had left when I left for my journey. The Prince of Darkness already knew that I belonged to the Prince of Light; and where the Father would allow me to go the Lord would never leave me. I would be going to a camp for spiritual warfare, learning to fight for my family (the church). So the enemy packed up and took his disciples with him and left my home. He knew my Father would have the victory, and he did.

As sweet as honey, the journey has brought us closer. I challenge all the saints all over the world to ask themselves, "Who is my Father? Am I a child of God or a child of the devil?"

Know that you can only have one Father and be tested, and it will be then you will know who your

Father truly is. All the prophets were tested, and you will need to be also, so when you are feeling like the Father and the Son of God *do not answer,* you are being DNA-tested.

Moreover, if you want to be a match for the kingdom of God, you need to be still so that Satan's temptation does not claim you. And if you are wondering how my journey ended, I will tell you what the Father told me: "I will seal up what you have written. No one will know their ending because it is determined by God, but yet! They will overcome evil by the blood of the lamb and by the word of their testimony (Revelation 12:11); and if you find yourself not believing, there is a heavenly Father."

A heavenly host, a creator of all things! Just look up, for since the creation of the world, God's invisible qualities—his eternal power and his divine nature—have been clearly seen and understood from what has been made so that men are without excuse.

Everyone knows there is a living God (Romans 1–20), and the voice of the Son speaks in every soul, teaching us wrong from right. He is the Christ, the Morning Star. He is the one who walks among the seven golden lampstands (the churches) and who holds the seven stars in his right hand (the angels), and he knows our deeds.

For those known as his loved ones and for those not known as his loved ones, the Father says, "You are my people." And we will all say, "You are my God."

The word of the Lord brought charges against us, for there is little faithfulness and love in the church.

Why? When the Father sent seven angels to earth for the churches to pave the way, for those without love, Ephesus-hearted, he sent the apostle John. For those persecuted for righteousness, Smyrna, he sent John the Baptist. For the compromising, always compromising the law of the land, Pergamum, he sent Moses. For the corruption trying to serve God and mammon, Thyatira, he sent the prophet Elijah. For the dead inside, spiritually dead Sardis, he sent the prophet Isaiah. For the faithful and true, Philadelphia, the Messiah himself came down from heaven to all who believe, faithful with unfaithful believers with unbelievers. For the neither-hot-nor-cold, always-in-danger-of-death Laodicea, he sent the prophet Jeremiah.

With repentance, we must turn from our wicked spirit of prostitution. Church we are living in a fallen world. Fallen! Fallen! Is Babylon the Great! She has become a home for demons. And a haunt for every evil spirit. Pray and keep watch!

(Revelation 18:2) Amen.

> This is for the man at the altar
> The messengers of the churches
> The woes are coming
> Let him who does wrong continue to do wrong
> Let him who is vile continue to be vile
> Let him who does right continue to do right
> Let him who is holy continue to be holy
> Revelation 22:11